The Lives and Loves of Jesobel Jones

Anna Mainwaring

The Lives and Loves of Jesobel Jones

For Grace and Beth
And my twenty-nine extra daughters

Chapter 1

Invisible Rule № 1: Being a girl sucks. And blows. All at the same time.

So it's a Tuesday morning in May and me – Jess – and my best mates, Izzie and Hannah, are in our fave place: the cellar of Hannah's house. Which would normally make us happy.

But not today.

Tuesday, May 3rd.

Today is Own Clothes Day, the most nerve-wracking day of the year.

That's Izzie in front of the mirror, putting on her fourth coat of mascara. She's going for the wicked-fairy-who's-fallen-on-hard-times look, but amazingly she seems to pull it off.

I stare at her perfect straight dark hair, I admit, with a touch of jealousy. She looks like someone out of the magazines that lie abandoned on the floor around us.

"You'd never guess you were a Man City fan until three months ago," I say.

Izzie humphs. She doesn't like to be reminded that she's made the bizarre transition from football fan to white witch. Not quite like Jadis in Narnia – we're a bit short of polar bears and sleds round here – but she does think she can do magic. Worse still, most of our school believes her. But this means that she can go for the emo look and no one will hate her for it.

Next to her, with the dark red hair and pale complexion – that's Hannah. She's more conventionally dressed in a series of cunning layers that bring her in at the right places and out and up at the right places. With her big eyes and ringlets, she looks a bit like a Disney princess. But whereas Disney princesses are never famous for having much going on between their ears, Hannah is on course for eleven A*s in her GCSEs.

Clearly not just a pretty face . . .

Hannah turns round and stares at her backside.

"Do my slag lines show?" she asks.

I look closely, as only a best friend can at another friend's arse. "Nope," I say, "you pass the slag test."

She smiles contentedly and goes back to work on her eyebrows. She's going for the Scouse Brow today. I'm saying nothing, but in a few minutes, it'll look like two slugs are sitting on top of her eyes. I blame those magazines. For an intelligent girl, she clearly doesn't mind drawing on fake eyebrows that make her look – well TBH – a bit stupid.

Then there's me. Jesobel – Jess for short. I sort of like my name cos it sounds pretty. But older people always look shocked when they're introduced to me. Apparently the original Jezebel was some kind of witch from the Bible who got executed for doing magic and then her dead body was fed to the dogs. Nice.

Whilst nothing that bad is likely to happen to me, I can't say that I'm that happy ATM. I look in the mirror and, well, sigh. I don't quite look myself in the eye cos I'm not perfect and I don't look like I've just wandered out of a GHD advert. Girls like me don't get to be in magazines.

I'm just getting changed cos apparently what I'm wearing just won't do, according to my fashionista friends.

"You're Year Eleven! That's what Year Nine will be wearing!" Hannah cries.

I look down at my so-called skinny jeans and Hollister top. She has a point – I have been wearing the same outfit for the last two years. (Don't worry, it has been washed – I don't mean LITERALLY wearing it for two years – that would be gross.)

Izzie grabs my holdall. "Let's see what else you've got. Did you bring the leggings?" She rummages through it, tossing one garment aside and then grabbing the next with glee. "Yes!" she cries, and I'm sent to the corner to change clothes. Apparently T-shirt, waistcoat, short skirt and leggings are *so* much better than what I had on before.

I look in the mirror. Yup, I'm still exactly the same person – no magical transformation yet. My mum, self-styled MILF and part-time hand model (FYI that *is* a real job), would still look at me and sigh with disappointment.

But I do think I look better. And I do want to look nice, I really do, I just find it difficult to find clothes that suit me. Apparently there are RULES for what you should wear if you're a bit, well, aesthetically challenged.

Yes, readers, I'm not thin. I am, in fact, a bit overweight. Some might say fat, and on a bad day I'd agree with them. I'm not a whale, mind, just, you know, curvy. And curves are good, aren't they? Magazines are always telling us that, but for them, curves seem to be just one step up from stick thin. My idea of curves is having boobs that actually wobble when you run upstairs . . .

And most days my wobbly bits don't bother me cos I like to go my own way, I don't like to be like everybody else.

But some days are harder than others.

Today, for example.

You might be wondering why there's so much fuss over what we're wearing and you know, I'm kind of with you on this one. But then again . . . let's think it over for a minute.

Take an all-girls' school and stick it in a reasonably posh area – South Manchester – stuffed full of WAGs, doctors, dentists, lawyers, TV presenters, artists, who all want their darling daughters to be the BEST. It's like the *Hunger Games* without the bows and arrows – a fight to the death to be the cleverest, thinnest, prettiest, most popular girl in the school.

That's just on a normal day. Own Clothes Day is worse, much worse. Every detail of what we wear will be noted, analysed and posted on Facebook within seconds of us arriving at school, accompanied by mean comments if we've got it wrong.

So, I wish it was tomorrow already. Or that a freak snow day would close us down for the day . . .

But that's not going to happen . . . cos it's May. And anyway, now that I'm dressed, I'm feeling a bit hungry and thinking that food might get the day off to a better start.

"I know what will make things just tickety-boo," I say. (I know it's an old-fashioned word. I was brought up mostly by my grandmother. This shows from time to time.) I pick up the plastic container that I have carefully carried from my house, two streets away, and tease open the lid.

Izzie and Hannah simultaneously sigh as if they have both just seen the most beautiful sight in the world. Which they have, even if I do say so myself.

Because in front of them is perfection in edible form. In an ordinary plastic container are three perfectly baked and perfectly crafted cupcakes. Izzie may be a witch who can do love potions that actually work, Jess may be able to read a Jane Austen novel in one sitting, but I am the queen of the cupcake. The sponge is light, the frosting is the most delicious blend of butter and icing, the faint dusting of confectioner's glitter is artfully applied: a true balance of skill and deliciousness. I bask in the glory of my art.

Trouble is they're not low fat, low carbs or low anything. But then I'm a full-fat kind of girl.

What happens next is what normally happens when girls are faced with one of my creations.

There is a struggle.

Hannah looks as if she's in actual physical pain. "They're lovely, but I shouldn't," she sighs.

Izzie stares at me. "I suppose there's no point in asking how many calories?"

"Don't know, don't care," is my normal response to that question. I don't generally use the C word, as I like to call it. (But around 450 each, if you really want to know.)

Her hand hovers out and then comes back. "I could skip lunch, I suppose."

I nod encouragingly as I grab a cake and take a bite. Leaning back into the old sofa, I enjoy the explosion of creamy sweetness as it hits my taste buds.

Izzie gives in first. "Oh, they're just so lovely – and I did go to the gym last night." She giggles and gasps as she takes her first bite. "Better than ever, Jess," she breathes.

Hannah's dilemma is written all over her face. She's picked up a cake but she's just gazing at it, listening to the voice in her head telling her to Put It Down.

"I'll have it if you don't want it," I say to test her out.

"No," she squeals, "no, I want it!" And she starts to stuff it down her, as if she's terrified I might grab it.

As she eats I do feel a moment of satisfaction – *Cupcakes–1, Fear of Being Fat–0*.

I know what you're thinking – we're girls and food is bad because food makes us fat. Then we'll have no friends so we might as well kill ourselves now. That's the invisible rule, isn't it? If you're a teenage girl, you should hate your body, hate food and hate yourself.

Well, I don't think like that.

I don't get why food is the enemy. I think food is good because it's nice to eat. Have you noticed that people are often nicer when they're sitting around eating and talking, rather than not eating and being miserable? Yes, Cat, if you ever get round to reading this, I do mean you.

And also food never lets me down. It's always there and always makes me feel good. And there aren't too many things you can say that about.

Anyway . . . cakes eaten and clothes sorted, it's on to hair and make-up and, within seconds, the cellar is full of the familiar smells of teenage girls: scorched hair, body spray and scented lip-gloss.

Finally Hannah smiles. "Okay, we're fine for time and we all look great. Result."

We stare at our reflections in the old, mottled mirror that hangs on the wall of the cellar. I pull myself together and, for once, I look myself in the eyes and I think, you know, it could be worse. I'm not all that, but the mirror hasn't cracked. My mum might think I'm fat, my sister might think I'm fat – hell, most of the school thinks I'm fat, but I still have friends and my life is pretty much okay.

And anyway, this is my choice. I could always lose weight if I wanted. Which I don't. Do I?

"Come on, time to go," Izzie says, and that's that. Deep breath, off to face the day ahead.

Let the games begin . . .

Chapter 2

Invisible Rule № 2: If a girl has curly hair, she wants straight. If she's short, she wants to be tall. If she's got no boobs, she wants huge ones. You're never allowed to be happy with what you've got. FML.

We head down the high street as slowly as possible. No one wants to look too keen, and the walk to school is the best opportunity, today of all days, to see who's wearing what and whether anyone is really way out there. Like the year Sonia Fitzherbert came wearing her mum's wedding dress and full white body make-up. Apparently, she was being some weirdo from some book by Dickens, who never got over not getting married. WTF. Clearly online dating didn't exist back in the dark ages.

As a team, Hannah, Izzie and I attempt to check out Ruth Mulholland and Sara Ejaz, also from our year, who walk parallel to us on the other side of the road. They look at us, we look at them. We're wearing the same kind of stuff. But not exactly the same. No, apparently that would be the Worst Thing That Could Happen. I just don't get some of these rules.

Anyway, we wave at each other and give a thumbs up. Cos we try to be nice. Whereas we know that other girls will just do THE LOOK. You know, where they scan you up and down with a sour face like they've got a mouthful of Tangfastics, and you know they're doing a checklist of your faults.

Recipe For the Perfect Girl (according to people who read too many magazines):
1. *Legs* – thigh gap – check. Also absolutely NO sug-

gestion that hair ever grows on these babies at all. Ever.

2. *Boobs* – need to look like small firm jellies that point up, absolutely NO hint of nipples.
3. *Skin* – airbrushed perfection.
4. *Hair* – must look natural in a way that only three hours before a mirror and twenty products can create.
5. *Stomach* – flat and hard enough to roll pastry on.

I could go on – but I can't bear to.

Far more interesting are two boys from the boys' school who are our FRIENDS but not our BOYFRIENDS. We are invited over by those most romantic words, "Hey, wenches."

Dominic Hall and Fred Cormack are lounging on a bench. We've known each other for years. In fact, I married Dom in the Wendy house one lunchtime back in Year Two, so I'll assume that the "wench" comment is ironic. But we do fool around at parties if there's no one else we fancy. I like him, but he doesn't make my heart race.

"Looking good, girls," Dom says as he checks us out, up and down, apparently appreciating all our efforts.

"Of course," Hannah says with a well-practised flick of her hair, "we always look good."

Which is weird. Even with our friends-who-happen-to-be-boys, Hannah has suddenly changed from a normal person into a strange, smirking, hair-flicking robot.

"So, did you hear about . . ." Fred leans in with the latest news. Boys may *say* they don't gossip, but they're just as bad as us.

But while I'm half listening to what Girl B might have done or not done to Boy A, I can't help thinking about all the time we three have put into our appearance this morning (the clothes, the hair, the make-up), when Dom and Fred have clearly just squirted on the Lynx and they're good to go. I don't think Fred has even brushed his hair. This year. Dom has spots. But whereas a girl would struggle to leave the house without twenty layers of concealer on them, Dom clearly still loves himself. If reincarnation does exist, I want to come back as a boy. At least then, when I fart in public, everyone will find it funny.

Then I notice how Dom stares at my boobs. There are a variety of ways to look at this.

a) I'm getting male attention. In public, for all to see. Which is good and makes me look good in the eyes of all the girls walking past, who WILL be taking notice.

Or

b) How rude – there is more to me than my mammary glands. But given that I am, you know, on the large side, some girls would think that I'm lucky to get any guy to notice me. Weirdly, it's girls who give me grief for being fat, not boys.

"You *can* look at my face, you know," I say to him.
He laughs and hits me on the arm.

"Sorry," he says, "but I'm a boy. I'm just a testosterone machine, hard-wired to look at breasts. And yours are just amazing. Are you absolutely sure that you've not had a boob job this year?"

I sigh and then I blush more than just a bit, not sure how to take this. I mean, this is good, isn't it? But do I want to be liked just for some random genetic factor that means I've not seen my feet for the last year?

"How many times do I have to tell you? I haven't had a boob job – all my hormones just kicked in at once!"

"Well, my hormones like what your hormones are doing to your body," he says cheerfully, punching me on the arm to show that this is just JOKING and not FLIRTING. I think. Or am I missing something?

As he turns back to the others to catch up with the latest, I carefully scope round to see if a certain boy is there. A boy who makes my heart, face and other parts of my anatomy tingle if I see him. You see, I have a bit of a secret crush on this guy called Matt Paige. Who unfortunately is not in sight today.

I do mean *secret*. I would actually rather die than tell anyone. And I do mean *crush* because the amount of time I think about him puts me into the category of Scary Stalker Girl.

And this is how it happened. How I fell ridiculously head over heels for him – just because of one second.

He lives near me. About a year ago, he was walking home and I was in my room, doing my homework in a distracted sort of way – well, I was just looking out of the window. And I looked down at him, he looked up at me.

And he smiled.

At me.

That was it. That was all it took. One second of him smiling at me.

All of a sudden, I realised that under that mad mop of hair, he was fit. With a good smile. And I sort of glowed inside. It was one of the first times ever that a boy actually looked at me and smiled. As if I was pretty and not just fat. It was lovely!

Of course, reality kicked in later and I realised that I'd been sitting down and so all he saw was my face. And if you just see my face, I don't look fat. If you just see my face, I look a bit like my mum. But I can't just be a face. The rest of me is attached. I can't push myself to school sitting on a wheelie chair with a desk in front of me to disguise the fatness.

But for months now, he's all I can think about. He's in Year Twelve at the boys' school, so he's an older man! You can tell a lot from a boy's A-level choices and his are: Psychology (in touch with his feelings), English Literature (you have to be a real man to do English at the boys' school – imagine the piss-taking), French (swoon) and, wait for it – Art (double swoon). What a combination – perfect or what? He's interested in human nature, he's creative, bilingual and actually confesses to reading books! I know all this because Hannah's elder brother, Alex, is in his year and she found all this out for me. It took me ages to ask all the right questions so that she told me everything without realising that I fancied him.

But I'm me and he's him and there's very little chance of anything happening. There might be if I looked a bit more like that girl over there – a vision of female perfection, lounging on a low wall, surrounded by tall, fit boys. All our group are suddenly staring at her.

She's the girl that every girl wants to be and every boy wants to have. She's thin, she's pretty, and she has those huge eyes that look too big for her face. She's wearing shiny leggings and manages that winning combination of sexy and vulnerable. The boys competing for her attention are perfect. Tall, hot, old, but not too old. And guess what? They look her in the eye. Not at her chest or her friends. At her. Because somehow, being attractive means that boys make more effort with you. *You're worth it.*

Her tinkling laugh chimes out and for a split second, her dark eyes break away from the group and lightly scan over us. I have a strange feeling when I look at her. I don't want to conform. A part of me just likes being that bit different and I don't want to be what everyone else thinks is normal. Yet I do want someone to look at me like that, as if I'm, you know, fit. More than that – worth looking at. But I can't help thinking that this might be more likely if I looked a bit less like me and a bit more like that girl over there.

Since I was little, I've watched all the Disney films, happy in the knowledge that all I have to do is to be myself and I will be loved. Except, in Disney films, "being yourself" also means being impossibly thin, with ridiculously large eyes and perfect hair. Not to mention a two-dimensional cartoon character.

A bit like that girl on the wall.

Dom sighs deeply. "She's so fit, your sister." He looks back at me and shakes his head, polite enough for once not to say what I've heard so many times, "How can you two be sisters?"

"Yeah, yeah, yeah," I say. "But Cat's out of your league."

"Not in my head, she's not." He grins wickedly and winks, and I'm not sure whether to be shocked or to laugh. I laugh – it's generally the best way to deal with whatever life throws at me.

Time is moving on. According to the big clock over the row of shops, we have seven minutes to get to school. If we move up a gear from dawdle to walk, we'll get there in time. The boys drift off, casting longing looks at Cat. She doesn't look at me again. She pretty much ignores me all the time. This has being going on for about a year, since around the time she stopped eating. I wish I knew why, but I don't.

Hannah catches my eye and I shrug. We've talked about Cat so many times that there's nothing more to say. But as we stroll up the hill to school, I do fantasize about force-feeding her a whole plate of my very best cupcakes until she balloons to – OMG – my size. Would boys still look past me to her the way they do now?

As I'm about to enter the school gates, Hannah puts a warning hand on my arm.

It's Mrs Brown, Assistant Head with special responsibility for Child Intimidation, standing by the main entrance. She can normally be found striding down corridors like the Snow Queen, sucking the life-spirit out of all who cross her path. I swear even teachers hide behind corners to get away from her.

I'm not usually so horrible, but she is the nastiest person who ever lived. It's not just that she's mean, but that she seems to enjoy being mean. The more the Year Sevens cry when she screams at them when they forget to button up their blazers (I know, what a terrible crime – an undone button!!!) the more she smiles. And there are no rules against a teacher who bullies children, other teachers and parents.

So there she is, standing guard at the gate, nostrils flared, looking for trouble, sniffing out anything that's visible that shouldn't be. Cos that's one of the many things that drives her crazy – female flesh on show. Just behind her, her latest victims stand cowed. Their crimes are easy to guess. Quivering Amy Dutton? Too much cleavage. Snivelling Julie Macdonald? Midriff visible. Defiant Catherine Temple? Skirt like a belt. Likely punishment for dressing like this? Being banned from the end of year Prom. And that means that their social lives have just died.

Just as we get close, one of the younger teachers walks past. Mrs Brown's eyes rake her like a laser, taking in the pencil skirt, the high heels and the fitted cardigan. I see her eyes narrow. "Miss Farrow. See me after registration," Brown bellows.

Poor Miss Farrow bites her ruby lips and looks petrified. We sigh for her. She'll learn. Even female teachers have to avoid any suggestion that they might be vaguely attractive women. Not that I really want to go there – I mean they're *teachers*, after all.

As we rush past Mrs Brown, we hear an intake of breath as she looks at Izzie, but we're saved. A scream and a whimper break out behind us.

"Charlotte Harrison, are those FISHNET tights? FISH-NETS? Get yourself over here."

And another is sacrificed so we can go free. For the moment.

Izzie sighs. "She'd prefer it if we all wore burkas and then nothing would be on show."

"We wouldn't even be safe then," I reply. "Remember Safia Iman? Brown got rid of her just cos her headscarf wasn't in school colours."

So it's 8.49 a.m. and we seem to have survived so far.

But I speak too soon because as we climb up the stairs to our form room, Izzie spots danger ahead. "Oh no," she says, "here they come."

And the next trial begins.

So we've just got past the psychopath teacher. Well, now meet the students who are most like her. Just a bit prettier.

Meet Zara, Tara, Lara, Tilly and Tiff.

I could try to describe their individual characteristics but they all get confused in my head. Just imagine some kind of many-headed Hydra from a horror film, each snake's head with perfect make-up and straightened hair. Once upon a time I was quite friendly with Lara. But this was before she discovered Tara and Zara, and their personalities merged and all Lara's nice bits got lost in the mix.

Let me sum them up:

1. They stalk through the corridors as if on a catwalk, trailing perfume, money and attitude as they pout and pose, making lesser girls leap out of their way.

2. They talk loudly so everyone has to overhear all the precise details of their interactions with boys, all designed to make you feel inferior if your last close encounter with an attractive member of the opposite sex was buying a skinny hot chocolate in Starbucks.
3. They tease you if you haven't had sex #virgin.
4. They tease you if you have had sex #slut.
5. They don't like anyone. Heck, I don't think they even like themselves.

They file past us on the stairs, sniggering.

"Nice look, Izzie," Tara simpers. "You'll need a love potion to get anyone to fancy you in that get up."

Hannah they merely ignore.

Zara checks me up and down with a deliberate stare. "My oh my, we all know you like your food, Jess, but it's really starting to show."

"Nice, Zara," I say, and as they walk on, giggling, I shout out, "Oh by the way, you should ask Tilly what she was doing with Jamie in the park last night." (Mean, but true – you have to use whatever ammunition comes your way.)

Zara spins round, her eyes like a snake, while poor Tilly begins to quiver. My days, is she going to be in trouble later!

Then Zara lightly runs down a few steps and stands, staring, over me. "You fat cow," she hisses and I laugh in her face and turn away from her. I'm not quite sure what happens then. Does she push me? Does someone push her into me? All I know is that I'm flying backwards and I land hard on my backside.

"At least you have a soft landing," Zara purrs and as she turns, she flicks a glance back over me. "As I said, it's starting to show."

I look down and see that my leggings have ripped at the seam, from halfway down my thigh to my calf, revealing a huge expanse of white flesh. Zara stares at me in triumph and waltzes off. Well, at least waxing my legs last night was a good idea.

Even so: *Bullies–1, Jess–0.*

Chapter 3

Invisible Rule № 3: If a pupil doesn't do their work, they get detention. If a teacher doesn't mark work, nothing happens. There is no such thing as teacher detention.

Hannah sits down next to me on the stairs as I rub my sore backside.

"Are you all right?" she asks. "Shall we tell Mrs Carroway?"

I give her a Look. "I'm not going to a form tutor about anything. We are not Year Sevens. I'll get my own back on her somehow, don't you worry." With that, I hoist myself back up, my ego hurting more than my bum, and that is killing me.

Other girls filter past, some with soft whispers, others calling out, "Okay, Jess?"

Sporty Amy T jogs by. "Don't worry, Jess, I've got General PE with Zara this afternoon. I'll take her down then! She can run but she can't hide." She trots on with a wink.

The three of us look down at my ripped leggings. The intake of breath from Hannah and Izzie confirm that it's worse than I thought.

"Textiles?" Izzie says hopefully, but I can see straight away that the material is too frayed to sew back together properly. There is just a sea of bare white leg. I didn't think the leggings were *that* tight.

Then, a thought that's been buzzing round my brain gets louder and clearer. What if – I can't believe I'm actually thinking this – what if Zara is right? What if I am actually getting too fat? What if I've just gone from "Well I can just about live with that" to "We don't stock your size here. Why don't you try the FAT shop next door for FAT people?"?

While I'm thinking the unthinkable, my friends are attempting to sort out my life. "Let's ask around. Someone's bound to have something spare to wear, and leggings, well, they fit anyone," Izzie says helpfully.

I look at the legs filing past and notice, more bitterly than I normally would, that they're all a lot thinner than mine. I know there are lots of fat people in the world. Just not round here. No, this area seems to be a fat-exclusion zone, with big signs showing a crossed-out large person eating a cake – *FAT PERSONS NOT WELCOME HERE.*

The school bell rings and now we're officially late for registration but that's okay because Mrs Carroway is ALWAYS late. So I go to the toilets and take off the leggings. I wish I'd worn my jeans. As I look in the mirror, I feel horribly exposed. This skirt is too short to wear without tights or leggings. I can live with my legs when they're covered up. But *au naturel*? I think not.

The door of the loos bangs and who should come in but Catamaran Caroline (so-called because she was once over-heard saying "Daddy's thinking of buying a catamaran this weekend" in the same way your or my dad might think of buying a Meatloaf album. In case you don't know, a cata-maran is some kind of weird boat that not even idiots can capsize. They cost A LOT). She gives me the once-over, then makes a face like she's seen some sick. How many more peo-ple are going to look at me like that today?

As a result of all this, I am three minutes late for registra-tion.

And guess what? Just for once, just because this is clearly the day when all the Bad Stuff is going to happen, Mrs Car-roway's on time. She usually swans in ten minutes late with a Starbucks in her hand, but today she's already sitting at the computer, logged on and ready to go. She attempts to give me (queen of the stare) a hard stare.

It fails.

My spirit is unsquashed. She starts calling out the messag-es for the day and doesn't seem to notice the amount of leg that I'm unwillingly showing. So I just sit down.

But Mrs C clearly got out of bed the wrong side. "Jesobel, it's not like you to be late. I'll let this one go but you'll be get-ting a letter home if it happens again."

Oh God, I'm quaking in my Converses. A LETTER. In the

Twenty-first Century, the school attempts to communicate our sins to parents via paper letters. They don't seem to notice that no one ever replies to these letters. Because parents never actually get them. Cos we steal them. So there you go – *School–0, Pupils–1.*

My other friends try to offer help. There's Sana – small, huge eyes, constantly readjusting her headscarf. Then Suzie – funny, long legs, never hands her homework in on time. Finally, Bex. She finds school hard. She finds life hard. But even she feels sorry for me today.

The bell rings. So, with legs still scarily exposed, it's off to English. I hope it's not one of those lessons where you're made to put Post-its on the board.

There are generally two kinds of teachers – young ones who've been on courses and try and make you do stuff in an "interesting" way, and old ones who just get on with it with as little fuss as possible, unless the inspectors are in. Fortunately Mrs Lewis is one of the old ones. She just puts some questions on the board and leaves us to work through them, so my legs can stay safely hidden behind my desk.

Unfortunately, this gives her time to check who's done their homework.

"Jesobel, I'm still missing an essay from you from last week."

I wince. What I really want to say is, "I'll give it in when you mark my controlled assessment, which you've had for four weeks." I mean, I'm in trouble for not doing my work but I'm not allowed to say to her, "That's not good enough, Mrs Lewis. You're in detention."

I just don't buy that line teachers give us about being so busy. I whisper to Izzie, "Funny how when we walk past her house, she's always drinking white wine and watching *Come Dine With Me.* Busy, my aching arse!"

I think I whisper this too loudly, because now Mrs Lewis is looking at me as if I've just said Shakespeare is a bit overrated.

"What did you just say, Jesobel?" she snaps.

"I was just saying how moving I found this poem," I lie. Then I put on the wounded puppy expression. "Sorry about the homework, miss, I'll hand it in tomorrow."

"I expect better from one of my prefects," she says sharply.

And I feel like screaming, cos today's been quite trying and it's not even nine o'clock yet. But I smile sweetly while I imagine her drowning in a vat of crisp white wine, her little arms waving as she bobs pathetically, sinking deeper and deeper into the alcohol. Just cos I'm a prefect – a dubious honour at the best of times – I'm supposed to be bloody perfect.

"Well," she says with a cold smile, "if I can't mark your work, I can't tell if you're on target for your predicted grade. So you'd better go and sit with the girls who are below target."

The whole class draws in a deep breath.

Thing is, in our school, you sit in order.

Those who are pretty perfect and who have nice stationery and handwriting and are going to get As or A*s are in one group. I'm always in this group. I'm not proud of it – I just like those novelty rubbers. Then there are the more normal guys who are going to get Bs and, hell, maybe a few Cs. And there's the rest – Ds or below. They look sad, like rescue puppies that no one wants. This system is supposed to encourage us/shame us to stay out of the bottom group.

I can feel words bubbling up inside me like lava in a volcano. But I don't say a word. I just move myself, my books, my bag, my pencil case with all its lovely colour-coded pens, and sit down at the Fail Table. With Ellie Unwin, who smells, and not in a nice way. And Rosie Sherwood, who cries all the time. Just great.

So by now, I'm beginning to feel a bit stressed. Let's review the situation.

1. I'm wearing a skirt that makes me feel ridiculous #fashionfail.
2. Most days I don't feel fat. Today I do.
3. The levels of hypocrisy and double standards today have gone from "mildly annoying" to "this place is driving me crazy".
4. I'm just a bit tired of being made to feel like rubbish by people whose opinions normally don't

matter to me.

5. I generally seem to have lost my mojo for a bit. I want my mojo back! #wheresmymojo.

So does any of this explain what happens next? Because what happens next is this – it all goes tits up on the way to Music.

Chapter 4

Jess Observation № 1: Doing what you're told is sometimes over-rated.

TBH, the rest of that English lesson is hard. Not academi-cally hard, just, you know, *hard*. Okay, I get sympathy looks from the rest of the class apart from Tilly, who looks as happy as if she'd just squeezed herself into a pair of size six jeans and the zip didn't burst. I can see her secretly tapping away on her phone and I just know she's spreading all this back to Zara, the many-headed queen of evil. A bit of me just wants to have a bit of a cry.

But I don't.

I just get on with it.

I feel that I've done a lot of just getting on with it lately. I also begin to feel that I would like to do more than "just get-ting on".

So I put my head down and answer a serious of devious questions on a poem that seems to me to be a random swirl of words on a page but apparently is a work of genius cos some dead white guy wrote it.

Another thing that stops me crying is that Ellie and Rosie, my fellow public failures, really can't do this. I know the BS that the exam board wants and can normally happily puke up pages of it, but Ellie is chewing her pen in a sad sort of way and adding smiley faces to all the i's in her work while Rosie is weeping into her homework planner. I push my book so that Rosie can see it and nod to her to copy it. She almost smiles but not quite.

Meanwhile, on the non-failing tables, Sana chats away to Bex for pretty much all of the lesson and so keeps Mrs Lewis's attention away from us and our cheating. Note to any teach-ers out there – don't worry about the noisy ones, they're easy to spot. It's the quiet ones you need to watch.

The bell screeches at the end of the lesson, soon drowned out by the sound of stationery being flung into bags. Izzie comes and stands next to me, making a sad face.

"I'll curse her if you like," she offers.

"You'd do that for me?" I laugh. "You're so sweet. Can I order boils or being hit by lightning?"

"You laugh at me," Izzie says, "but you know what I can do."

(Once she did a talk in English about a "love potion" and gave it to Rebecca Turner. Who then snogged Jay Hudsworth at a party. Yes, Rebecca Turner – not cool – snogged Jay Hudsworth – way cool. Izzie puts it down to her love potion. I put it down to vodka. The rest of the school is undecided. Though in this age of madness, I do think Izzie has more followers on this one than I do.)

We wander off into the main corridor, knocked about like corks in the sea as we are hit by a series of large bags carried by Year Sevens. The size of their bags seems to increase in direct proportion to their smallness. I'm sure you could turn this into a mathematical equation – which would then be the only useful thing done in a Maths lesson this century.

Izzie stops to chat to someone while I plough on up the stairs to Music. I'm not really in the mood for chitchat. I'm in the mood for an argument.

As I stand at the top of the steps, I see my reflection in an ancient glass cabinet. I see my legs in all their glory. Yuk. I really am half dressed. In fact, I have unwittingly achieved the slut look that half of Year Eleven aims for on a Friday night. I look like I should be in some music video, pumping, grinding and generally getting my groove on.

"Wicked look," Sana calls, and gives me a wolf whistle. I do a little shimmy in return.

"Work it, girlfriend," she continues and, giggling, I pretend that I'm on an imaginary catwalk, sashaying and spinning, blowing kisses to the invisible paparazzi. There's quite a few of us on the stairs and in the corridor, waiting to get into lessons, and the chant of "Go, Jess" begins to build as I continue to shake my thing.

Sana laughs as I spin and pout at her. She gets her phone out and starts to film me. "You got it, Jess!"

For the first time all day, I actually feel okay.

It's then I hear a cold laugh.

"Exactly what do you think you are doing, Jess Jones?"

I look down and see HER again. Zara. Her hair groomed to perfection, labels dripping off her skinny body. Everything I despise. Smirking as she looks up at me.

"How can you bear to look at yourself in the mirror?" she spits out. "You are just so fat now – you're grotesque."

My heart starts to pound. Everyone is watching now. Before, it was just a spat, but now I feel like everyone's waiting for me. To say something good. But my brain has stopped working. Because the things she is saying are the things that I say to myself sometimes. It's like that nasty voice inside your head that tells you all that's wrong with you. Only it's not *me* saying it this time. It's a nasty girl who thinks she can insult me just cos she's thin and I'm not.

I've had enough.

Adrenaline rushes through me and I'm spoiling for a fight. My backside still hurts and I've had a rubbish morning. All cos of her.

I stalk down the steps until I face her. I can sense a few others just behind me.

"Grotesque, Zara?" I hiss. "That's a big word for you – do you think you can spell it?"

She starts to speak but I stop her.

"I might be fat but I can change that if I want. But you, you will always be a bitch."

She starts forward – is she going for me again? God, this girl has anger issues.

But I'm not falling for it this time. So I just step back.

Which means that Zara, arm outstretched to slap me, pull my hair or some other girly form of physical abuse, flies through the air and lands on the floor at my feet.

"Hurrah," I say in mock triumph. "Fat girls–1, Bullies–0." And I put my foot on her arse before she has time to move, pumping my arms like I've just won a boxing match. Which I suppose I have, sort of.

Around me, there are a few cheers and whoops. Zara turns, pushes my foot from her, leaps to her feet, her face twisted in fury, mascara starting to run down her face in dirty rivers.

I almost feel sorry for her. But she did push me earlier and she would have done it again. I just got out of the way.

"I'll get you for this, Jess Jones." With that, she shoves her way through the crowd, Tilly and Tiff trailing behind her.

I look up at the small crowd on the stairs.

"Okay – show's over, people."

Most girls are laughing, smiling, giving me the thumbs up.

"Nice one, Jess, you showed her for once," Sana says. But I can't help noticing that Hannah hasn't said a word.

"She deserved it," I say defensively.

"I know," Hannah says, "but it just didn't feel like you just then."

I grimace. I know what she means. I'm not one of the bad guys normally. But that – that felt like I was being Zara and she was being me.

And this thought occupies me during most of Music and then break.

And then, later, when everyone around me is telling me I did well but I'm not so sure, that's when I hear the shout of doom.

"Jesobel Jones. Get. Yourself. Here. Now."

Chapter 5

Invisible Rule № 4: If you really, really don't want to do what a teacher tells you, then there's not much they can do to you.

It's Mrs Brown, Assistant Head from Hell. She's standing a few feet away from me in the hall, where I'm waiting for the next joyous lesson of the day, and she's pointing to the place just in front of her feet. Without even meaning to, I automatically wander over.

At first I'm not sure exactly what she's going on about. As I stand in front of Mrs Brown, it's like standing in a wind tunnel. She screams, she yells, spit flies in my face, she goes red.

"You. Are. A. Nasty. Piece. Of. Work," she shouts. Apparently she can only communicate in one-word sentences when angry.

I turn to Hannah. Who looks back at me in shock.

"You. Are. A. Bully," she continues.

Okay, I think I need to introduce her to a concept called irony. I mean, she's calling ME a bully?

"I've got Zara Lovechild sobbing in my office, bruises covering her arms. You did this to her."

I try to say something.

"Don't deny it. I saw it on the school cameras."

Zara might have been sobbing in her office a few moments ago, but now she's standing just behind Mrs Brown and, through the messed-up make-up, she's smiling at me in triumph, and then putting her hands to her eyes in a show of mock tears.

"Did you or did you not call her a 'bitch'?"

"Yes, but—"

"I have no time for 'buts'. You verbally and physically assaulted a fellow pupil. Get to my office now. And while we are there, we'll discuss what you're wearing. Because to put it simply: You. Are. Too. Fat. To. Wear. That. Skirt. You look ridiculous."

And it's at this point, as I see Zara's look of triumph, that I have finally had enough. Two bullies are accusing me of bullying, when I was just standing up for myself. And now a fat woman is calling me fat.

End of.

And so I turn and walk away.

Then there's more screaming.

"Don't. You. Walk. Away. From. Me. Jesobel. Jones."

I keep walking.

"One more step and you'll be suspended."

I take three more for good measure. I might as well be committing suicide but I've just had enough of this place today. She's just pushed me over the edge.

And with this, I'm off and back up the stairs before she has a chance to wrestle me to the ground.

Even with a head start, I don't fancy my chances. But as I dash up the stairs, I sense bodies behind me. The students of the school are somehow managing to slow her down.

This is more exercise than I'm used to. Out of breath, I turn a corner and see a cleaners' cupboard. Hiding suddenly seems a good idea so I open the door and dive inside. A little Year Seven, coming down the corridor towards me with the most enormous bag I've ever seen, looks at me in surprise and I put my fingers to my lips as I close the door.

Inside my cupboard, I hear the drumming of feet – Brown is in full chase mode. I'm almost sad that I'm hiding in a cupboard. I would have liked to have seen her run. That must be an awesome sight.

"Did you see her? Did Jesobel Jones come this way?" the voice of Brown booms.

A trembly voice replies, "A girl ran that way, miss."

"Get. That. Ridiculous. Bag. Out. Of. My. Way. Now."

The footsteps fade away.

I peer out and smile at the little girl, who grins back as she waves her bag in triumph. *School–1, Brown–0.*

So the rest is easy. I quickly find the back stairs, run down the fire escape and out into the grounds. For a second, I review my options. Really, I just need to get out of here. I feel like I've done some kind of sadistic workout and my heart is still threatening to implode. Not to mention my brain. I can't just walk out through the school gate as we're all locked in during the day.

But there's always a way. I push the recycling bins next to the wall and climb up. The drop down on to the road looks a bit scary, but not as scary as going back inside. If I don't make a move, they'll find me.

So I kneel on the wall, then sit on my bum and let my legs swing down. I take a big breath. I drop down and then I'm standing on the pavement. On the wrong side of the wall. With no way back.

In the street, it's calm and quiet. Unlike me.

I look at my watch. 11.33. How can so much have happened since I got up this morning? What am I going to do?

In my pocket, my phone is going crazy but, for the moment, I have a very unusual craving for home. Dad won't be up yet, Mum will be at the gym. If I walk quickly, I might just have time to get home to watch some black and white film with Gran before she has her first whisky.

And, today, I think I might just join her.

Chapter 6

Jess Observation № 2: Ever noticed how childish adults can be?

In the quiet street outside the school walls, there are no cars, a few trees and more dog poo than is called for in any so-called civilised country. An old lady walks past and smiles at me.

I wonder how I appear to her. Do I look like some kind of fugitive from justice? Or a criminal or, worse, a bully? Or do I just look like what I am – a red-faced teenage girl with fat legs who's missing a pair of leggings?

My heart is still hammering away. I remember doing something about cardiac arrests in Biology and I wonder if that's what's happening to me. Quickly I check behind me. There are no bloodhounds tracking me down. Maybe some computerised probe has been sent to stun me, wrap me in industrial steel wire and drag me back to Brown the Bruiser to face instant trial. I feel like I'm in one of those futuristic films where anything could happen. I certainly don't feel like me.

For a moment, I lean against a tree and concentrate on my breath coming in and out. We did some lesson on relaxation once but the teacher just lost it cos Abbie Norman kept farting.

No one from school has come to find me yet. I have two choices right here, right now.

1. I can go back to school and face the consequences now.

2. I can go home and face the consequences later.

3. I can go into town, draw out my entire finances (£245.31), get on a train and see how far that gets me (I don't have a passport on me so that limits my options).

4. I can drop out of school and hang around some bus stops for the next year or two. Maybe have a kid or two and live on benefits. (If the *Daily Mail* can be believed.)

After a bit of thought, I decide that 2 suits me best at the moment. 1 is probably the most sensible but being sensible is clearly not a course that I'm following today. I'm going for crash and burn so I might as well do it in style. Decision made, I make for home by the quickest route.

My mind begins to play out this morning's events. I left home a prefect, a student considered sensible and capable. At some point during the morning, I crossed a line. I've been accused of being a bully. And then I talked back to the teacher. In other schools, this might be quite common. At our school, not so much. At our school, it's considered outrageous not to open a door for a teacher and throw yourself down face first so they can walk over your back.

And I didn't cross just any teacher. No – it was Brown, infamous for her outrages upon students and teachers. So I know that there will be penalties for this.

Part of me expects to see her staked out in front of the house with a black hat on her head, a noose in her hand and a smile on her face, ready to hang me from the nearest street lamp.

The more rational part of me knows that the phone call from school to home has already happened and it's just a matter of time before it catches up with me.

As I turn down my street, there's an empty space outside our house where Mum's car is normally parked, so she's at the gym (even though she's been running already) or "networking" with the SOWs (Skinny Old Women). Networking seems to involve the drinking of industrial amounts of Prosecco but it's a bit early for that. Dad's car's there but I suspect that he's not up yet. (He was once the guitar player in a nineties band that was a one-hit wonder. He's not like a regular dad.) But there's no strange car outside the house, therefore school have not tracked me back to my lair yet.

As I open the front door, I hear Lauren's voice. My little sister's on the telephone. With her hair clearly not brushed this morning, still in her grubby pyjamas, she has jammy toast in one hand (and mostly smeared over her face) and her dummy, snuggly and the house phone in the other. She is deep in conversation with whoever's at the other end.

"Granny smells of wee," she says with great confidence to

the persons unknown on the telephone. "And she's a poo poo head." I can hear the person on the other end of the phone speaking slowly but Lauren just keeps talking. "And she's lazy cos she never gets out of her chair. I don't like Granny cos she's mean to Alice and I don't like anyone who's mean to Alice." As she says this her face crumples and tears begin to form in the corner of her eyes. It's like she's read a book on *How to Make Grown Ups Feel Sorry For You and Therefore Do Everything You Want.*

Lauren's eyes well up, her mouth turns into an O and her shoulders start to shake. "She said Alice was silly and she had to stand outside. But it's cold outside and I can hear Alice crying. And it makes me SAAADDD . . ." This final word turns into a wail and she drops the phone in her misery. A disembodied voice starts to ask strident questions. I hang up ASAP and I hug Lauren while enormous sobs rack her little body and she snuggles into me, all warmth and snot. Gross, yes, but she's my little sister so it is sort of cute too.

"Do you know who that was on the phone?" I ask, hoping to calm her down.

She wipes her running nose on my shoulder. I try not to flinch. "Someone for Mummy. But I told them that Mummy was out."

"Was it my school?" I say.

"I don't know," she says sadly. "Was Alice outside? Will you let her in?" Fresh tears flood down her fat cheeks.

I sigh, stand up, open the door and shout, "Come in, Alice," to the empty street. Lauren's face is transformed. "Alice!" she shouts with excitement. "Come and play cafes with me."

And with that, she runs upstairs, dummy now firmly in her mouth, with her hand outstretched as if she's holding someone's hand.

Yep, you've guessed it. Alice is not real. And the reason that Lauren and Gran don't get on is because Gran thinks that we humour Lauren too much and keeps telling her that Alice doesn't exist. Which is true. Gran is a big fan of truth. In some ways, she's the only person in the family who thinks that way. It's kind of why I like her.

I jump as the phone rings again and, like a trained professional in the art of avoiding unwanted phone calls, I disconnect the phone, cos now it's either school or social services coming round to take Lauren away as she's clearly special. Above me, a huge photo of an attractive young woman peers down seductively at me.

"Hi Mum," I say.

It's a photo of her in her early twenties, at the height of her so-called modelling career. It's a bit weird looking at it cos you can see a bit of me there. The eyes are the same. But whereas Mum's face is all cheekbones and pout, I look like I've been slightly overinflated by some bicycle pump.

Mum doesn't do much full on modelling these days. She's found this niche for herself. You know those close-ups in nail or hand-moisturising products? Well, that perfect hand with manicured nails probably belongs to her.

"Having a good day?" I ask Mum.

She doesn't answer back. Obvs. It's a photo. Lauren's madness is clearly catching. Assuming that my parents haven't completely lost it and left a four year old at home alone, I decide to track down any random adults who might be hiding in the house.

Upstairs, I hear another phone vibrating, knocking into things upstairs. Dad. I peek round the door into his and Mum's bedroom (dangerous activity at any time – my parents still find each other attractive – eek! Frequent PDAs have to be endured) but thank God he's in bed, alone, and fast asleep. His phone is buzzing like a demented bumble bee, spinning round and round on the shiny surface of the bedside table. He grunts. I grab the phone, put in his PIN and turn the phone off.

He opens an eye. "Whatsgonon?" he mumbles.

"Nothing. You're just dreaming, Dad," I whisper.

He nods and closes his eyes again. I despair. Dad should be looking after Lauren, but he's clearly still hungover from some gig last night which means that Gran has been left in charge of Lauren. Which is a bit tricky cos she never comes out of her attic. Though clearly Lauren has been up there this morning, judging by her rant about Gran. (BTW Gran doesn't smell of wee – but she does smell of weed.)

I climb the steep wooden steps to the second floor where Gran hangs out. So yes, I do live in quite a posh house. Three floors, nice Victorian floors, original features etc., but this isn't my parents' house. No, it belongs to Gran. She calles my parents Fur Coat and No Knickers. I think what she means is that Mum and Dad like look like they're rich but it's all show. My mum calls Gran Saggy Tits, but only when Gran can't hear her.

I knock on her door.

"Come in," she calls with her firm voice, from deep within a cloud of smoke. I cough, take a deep breath of clean air and go and sit next to the open window. It's the only way to keep a clear head when visiting.

"Jesobel. Now what might you be doing at home on a school morning?"

See, there's nothing wrong with Granny's brain, despite the constant consumption of dodgy substances. Unlike her son, who's clearly addled when he's less than half her age.

"I walked out of school," I say bluntly.

Gran nods and takes a long pull at her roll-up. "Wise girl. I'm not sure of the need to go every day. It seems rather excessive really. I mean, how much can one actually learn at school? All it teaches you is to conform to an authoritarian regime."

I nod.

"Now," she says, "as you're here, you might as well make yourself useful. Scrabble or gin rummy?"

As you can tell from her choice of cigarettes, Gran is a bit alternative. She spent most of her life protesting about something. Nuclear power. Fascists. Men who treat women badly. Well, just men really. And now, she just stays in her attic, listens to Radio 4 sometimes and draws. Weird, abstract things, but kind of cool at the same time.

Gran peers at me. "So you just left school, then?" she purrs. "That's not like you. You appear to be quite the conformist these days."

"On the surface, Gran," I say, "but today I didn't feel like playing the education game."

"That's my girl," she says. "Teachers – load of inadequates

if you ask me. You only start really learning anything when you leave school. All these exams rot your brain."

This is all normal Gran stuff. She is not your typical gran. She looked after me when I was little, when Dad was still vaguely famous, and Mum and he just cruised round London and the rest of the world. If you think I'm a bit odd, you know, by not starving myself until I'm a stick girl, then Gran is partly responsible. She's always encouraged me to be different. Which I know is good. But sometimes it can be a bit hard and a lot lonely.

Just as I'm dealing out the cards, I hear the front door slam and then the sound I was dreading most.

"Jess!" Mum's voice thunders up the stairs. How can someone so thin make so much noise? "I think it's time we had a little chat."

Something about that voice kind of chills me to the core. It's the tone of disappointment. A bit of me does feel a little sorry for Mum. Sometimes. I mean, this is the woman who puts every ounce of energy, every day, into how she looks. She checks her reflection in any shiny surface that comes her way. Her idea of a blow-out is putting a second olive on her rocket salad. She was quite a success in her modelling days and married a rock star. And she's ended up with me. Mum likes self-help books but you can't find anything on Amazon along the lines of *I Was a Supermodel – My Daughter's a Whale*.

Granny looks at me. "Well, young lady, it would be rude to keep The Plastic One waiting." She winks. "Come and report back to me later." She takes another draw on her roll-up. "If you're still alive, that is."

Things are not tickety-boo just now.

Chapter 7

Invisible Rule № 5: When a parent says they want to "talk", it means they want to tell you off. They talk, you listen.

Mum's voice echoes up the stairs. "Jesobel, I know you're up there."

I expect Dad'll be awake by now. Nothing like the sweet tones of your beloved to bring you back from your dreams. I'm not quite sure what Dad's dreams are but I expect he's on stage somewhere in the early nineties and I'm pretty sure that illicit drugs will be involved at some points. And probably fit groupies – i.e. Mum. I think I'll stop now before I gross myself out.

As I pass Dad's bedroom, there's definitely movement. A second later, Dad, all ungelled hair and baggy boxers, pokes his head round the door.

"Stephen, get yourself down here and make yourself useful for a change," Mum calls, with more than an edge of acid to her voice.

Dad goes off sheepishly and reappears in some trackies and I can hear him follow me down. I see Lauren is sitting on the stairs outside her room, looking rather sad.

"Alice sent me out for answering back. I can go back in when I've spent ten minutes on the naughty step," she says.

I make a mental note to have a chat with Alice later.

But before that I have to face my mother.

There she stands, fuming, next to the huge black and white shot of her twenty years ago. You have to give it to her – she's not let standards slip. From a distance, she looks much the same as she does in the picture. Large-eyed, groomed to perfection, her perfect nails sitting on her slim hips, she winces as I stomp down the stairs. The thought of my wobbling bits sets her teeth on edge – this is a woman who likes to keep flesh strictly under control.

"Jesobel," she starts, "I've had an interesting phone call from school. Apparently you've now taken to bullying girls. Care to tell me what this is about?"

By now, Stephen, aka Dad, has made it downstairs but is still not quite awake, as he's got his hand down his trackies and is giving himself a good scratch.

"Stephen!" Mum spits out his name, and he remembers vaguely where he is and what is appropriate behaviour.

"It's a bit early," he mumbles. "What's with all the aggression?" and he ambles into the living room. I follow him. I think I need to sit down, so I throw myself on the sofa. Mum paces in after us, her heels clicking manically on the stripped pine floor.

"So?" she starts. "Shall we begin with what on earth you are wearing?" Her eyes rake down to my bare legs and back up again. "I know you like to make a point about . . ." she pauses for a second, "your appearance, but I have to say that what you're wearing is unsuitable. I mean, frankly, Jess, I don't want to be harsh but you do look ridiculous. What were you *thinking*?"

Okay, this is all just a bit too much. It's like I'm facing some horrible mutant cross between my mum and Mrs Brown. My eyes begin to prick with hot tears and I stare hard at the floor to keep my face like a mask.

"I mean, if you want advice on which clothes would, well, suit . . ." her voice begins to quaver for a moment, "suit someone who . . ."

"Is fat?" I offer up helpfully.

She glares at me. "Someone who chooses to look like you, then you only have to ask. I mean, I do actually know something about fashion."

There is a tense silence. She is either saying that I don't know anything about fashion or that she's hurt that I haven't asked her advice. Or both.

I say nothing.

She gestures to a long package, draped over a chair next to me. "You might want to look at that later. I bought it for you. It would suit you perfectly. But I'm not sure that I want you to have it now."

Dad clears his throat. "Well, I think Jess has the right to express herself through her clothes if that's what she wants to do."

Mum glares at him. "And say what, particularly, with that look?"

His face crumples. But, *Nice try, Dad*, I think, and we exchange smiles.

"Let's move on then," Mum says. "I still don't understand why you're sitting at home, half naked, when you should be at school. You start your GCSEs in a few weeks!"

She looks at me, Dad looks at me, Lauren has left her naughty step and is peering round the door at me. How can I explain what happened this morning, and how everything is getting just a bit too much for me?

I take a deep breath. "Well, I sort of fell over and split my leggings. Well, Zara Lovechild pushed me and then, later on, she started at me again, and that's when it happened."

Mum opens her mouth as if to say something but for once thinks better of it.

"I was going to borrow something to wear but everything kept going wrong. And then Zara was really rude to me and then she sort of fell over. And I might have said some stuff. And then Mrs Brown saw me and just started screaming at me. Calling me a bully, when she's the meanest bully around, but she's a teacher so you're not allowed to say that. And she wouldn't listen to me so I just had enough." My voice tapers off and I begin to feel like everything I've said sounds so pathetic and childish. But Dad's nodding and Mum actually seems to be listening.

Lauren's voice pipes up. "Mrs Brown sounds like a knob head if she's mean to you, cos you're the nicest person I know."

Dad chokes, Mum takes a deep breath and I know she's counting to three and thinking of her happy place like they teach her on her Self-visualisation courses.

"Lauren, sweetie, where did you hear that expression?" Mum asks and she almost sounds calm but not quite.

Lauren smiles her sweet, four-year-old smile. "Daddy calls Uncle Barry that all the time when he thinks I'm watching

CBeebies. Is a knob head a nice person or a nasty person, Daddy?"

Mum hisses disapproval under her breath but Dad begins to laugh. Really laugh. And then I giggle. And before you know it, Lauren is squealing on the floor, Dad has tears running down his cheeks and even Mum's taut face cracks a smile (but not across the forehead, cos of the Botox).

Of course, Mum is the first to pull herself together. But Dad is the first to speak. "So Jess told some tight-arsed—"

"Stephen!"

"—some interfering old bully, where to go," Dad continues. "And that's it."

"Sort of," I mumble.

"And then she left the school premises," Mum points out.

"I'd just had enough of it all," I say.

She stares at me. "You have been behaving oddly lately. Are you okay? It's a stressful time – perhaps I should take you to see my doctor. He did wonders for Maria Morrison's youngest."

I say, "I don't need Prozac. I need Zara Lovechild to chill out and teachers not to give me so much stress and leave me alone."

"Right on," Dad says. "You don't need doctors messing with your head."

Mum sighs. "We all have to go to a meeting tomorrow morning at the school. Nine o'clock with Mr Ambrose. Bullying doesn't sound like you, I know, but I think you'll have to apologise for all of this. I know it's not fair, but unfortunately the world's not fair. I heard what you said, but they say that they've got evidence of you bullying this Zara girl. And the camera never lies."

I can feel a burning sensation, a bit like I'm going to be sick. "But . . ."

I don't see what I've got to apologise for. But if my own mum won't back me, then what chance do I have?

Mum sits next to me and puts her thin hand on my plump knee. "Jess, all I want is for you to be happy. And lately I just feel that you're going down pathways that are making you sad."

I stay silent.

"I mean, you're always cooking. I know it's been our family tradition that you cook, but all the books, the meals – it's all getting a bit out of hand. And your leggings splitting. Don't you think that that might be a sign that perhaps you could think about losing a few pounds? I think you'd be happier if you just, well, took care of yourself a bit more."

Mum's voice sounds gentle but I feel the barbs.

"You think I should be like Cat and never eat and just be miserable all the time?"

"Well, no, but as you've brought Cat up, let's face it – boys are always showing interest in her, and that could be you if you just made more effort."

"So you think I'll be happier if there was less of me?"

"That's not quite what I said."

I take another deep breath and feel the bubbles of anger welling up in me. "Look, Mum, your idea of happiness and my idea of happiness are very different. I think what will make me happy is having good friends, doing something worthwhile and having a brain full of ideas, not turning myself into a plastic version of a person in a magazine who never has any deep thoughts at all, beyond *Does my handbag match my underwear?*"

The silence is icy. We both know that I've just described my mother. And I've shown that I have no respect for her, just as she has no respect for me.

I've gone too far.

For the second time this day.

But, like the first time, I was just being honest.

And, just like the first time, I don't regret it. I just don't think like Mum and I think I'm right and she's wrong. Just like with Mrs Brown.

"You need to think this over in your room for a bit. You needn't cook tonight. I'll do it." Mum dismisses me.

Lauren tries to give me a hug but Mum drags her away from me and I plod back upstairs to my room.

I've never felt more alone in my life.

Chapter 8

Jess Observation № 3: If being thin is so great, why are thin people always miserable?

I stomp up to my room and realise that it's hours before I will have any meaningful communication with the outside world. How do I fill the time?

I could turn my phone back on and see who, if anyone, is concerned about me. But, freakishly for a modern teenager, I don't want to see the response to this morning just yet. For a moment, it felt fantabulous to get one over on Zara, but Mum's burst my balloon now. And I still have this lurking feeling that I shouldn't have humiliated her like that. At least only a few people saw it, though everyone will be talking about it.

So I watch TV. Sort of. If you surf around, you can find some decent cooking programmes. I've got all of *MasterChef: The Professionals* on Series Record, so I find my favourite episodes and make notes on any recipes I've missed.

A few hours later, I'm hungry and the house seems quiet.

I am unhappy. I consider: *What makes me happy when everything is a bit pants?*

Food. The cooking of it and especially the eating of it.

I'm not sure that's going to work for me today, but there's nothing else to do so I head down to the kitchen. Dad's off out being cool somewhere, Mum's taken Lauren shopping probably, Gran never leaves her "suite" and Cat's at college. Not that you'd notice if she was here. It's like living with a pretty ghost who just drifts in and out of our lives.

I open the cupboards and see what there is. After a few minutes of rifling through ingredients and flicking through my books, I have a brainwave. I'm going to build a model of the school out of gingerbread and then eat it! That's tickety—

41

(I stop myself saying that. I sound like a weirdo.) Okay, so the gingerbread thing is an odd metaphor for the relationship between myself, food, school and power, but let's just go with it for a bit.

This is an epic project which keeps me busy for the rest of the afternoon. After three hours of measuring, mixing, baking, cutting and constructing, I stand back and look at my handiwork. The main school bit and then the six portacabins that smell in summer and let the rain in in winter. Green icing for the playing fields. And even a little ginger bread clock tower . A bit wonky but definitely a recognisable *campanile*. It looks *so* cool even if I do say so myself. I take a photo and leave the gingerbread school there for Mum. She'll have me put in some hospital for crazy people. "Well, Doctor, making buildings out of cake is hardly normal, is it?"

By now it's nearly the end of the school day. The guys will be heading home and I need to talk to them. I don't want to see my family. I want my friends. So I head off out of the house and let myself into Hannah's cellar, where it all started just a few hours ago. How can so much have happened in so little time? I put on the ancient two-ring hob that we use down here and begin to make hot chocolate for them when they get in.

I don't have to wait long.

Hannah and Izzie come through the door exactly thirteen minutes and fourteen seconds after the school bell would have rung. That is truly a world record – I'm impressed.

They stand there for a minute.

"OMG," Hannah gasps. You know, I'd expect better from someone who reads as much as she does, but clearly it's one of those days where no one does what they're supposed to.

Izzie comes and sits next to me on the non-reclining recliner. "Seriously, are you okay?"

"As in, have I gone mad?" I reply. "Not really, I just couldn't help myself. I think I was possessed."

Izzie looks up with interest.

"I was joking. Spirit possession is not the explanation for what happened!" I say before she gets any ideas. "So what's the word?"

"You've not seen?" Hannah says. "It's all gone mental.

You're all anyone is talking about at school, or at the boys' school. This is better than when that Maths teacher ran away with that boy in Year Ten."

I raise a sceptical eyebrow – it's a look I've perfected over the years. Seriously? Me? Being talked about like this? "I walked out of school. What's the big deal here?"

Izzie and Hannah exchange looks. "You don't know, do you?"

"I don't know what?" I say.

"About the clip?" Hannah replies.

They both start to laugh.

"You will not believe this," Hannah says and flips up the lid of her ancient laptop.

I have a bad feeling about this. What clip?

"How can you not have seen this?"

"I turned my phone off and didn't go on the computer. I wasn't in the mood," I say.

"Well, she says, "I think you'll be in the mood for this. You're everywhere. Look."

She's on YouTube. It's a clip called *Fat Girl vs. Mean Girl*. WTF?

She hits play.

OMG.

It's me. It's a film of me. And Zara. You see me and my face as she says something that you can't hear. And then you see me say, with added subtitles, what I said: *"Grotesque, Zara? That's a big word for you – do you think you can spell it?"* And then she lunges forward and I step to the side. She falls flat on her face. And there I am, with my foot on her bum, pretending to be a triumphant boxer. The girls all around are cheering me on.

OMG.

There's a clip of me.

On the internet.

There have been a few thousand views already.

My first reaction: that's brilliant.

My second reaction: now the world knows exactly how fat my legs are. Do I really look like that? Okay, I'm fatter than I thought.

For once in my life I am speechless.

I keep watching the clip play over and over again. Partly in disbelief, partly in pride, partly in shock at my legs.

Weakly, I say, "Who put it on with the subtitles?"

Hannah looks proud. "Oh, that was my idea. Do you like it?"

See, normally I would like it, but now I'm not so sure. It's all so public.

Izzie is talking but I can't hear what she's saying.

"So, have you been expelled?" she says again with excitement.

I shake my head. "I've been excluded for the day and I'm in with the parents for the appointment of doom at nine o'clock."

I sigh. We all sigh. We all know that this will not be fun.

But that was before the clip. I think that might change things somehow.

Izzie pipes up, "Do you want me to read your cards?"

I bite my tongue (a bit). "You know, I'm gonna give that a miss today."

"You just don't believe in me," Izzie says. Where's the violin soundtrack behind her when you need it?

I look her in the eye. "You, I believe in, because I can touch you and see you, but your magic – that's a no from me." Since when did I start quoting *Dragon's Den*? Exactly how weird am I getting? Don't answer, that's a rhetorical question.

Hannah changes tack. "Let's log on. You've got to see this." She knows my password and, seconds later, there's my page. It's mad – loads of messages from people I've never heard of or, in the past, have been too cool to know me.

Hannah says, "Well, you need to think before you say anything, cos people are gonna want something special from you."

Obvs!

"So my latest recipe for bouillabaisse isn't gonna cut it?" I say.

Izzie gives me a withering look. "Your obsession with food is just as weird as my interest in magic."

"Except food is real and essential for life," I say.

Izzie rolls her eyes. "I feel the same about magic."

I'm not sure how much more of this I can take and then I remember the gingerbread model of the school. I knew that was a good idea.

Seconds later, I've posted the photo on Twitter and Facebook. Underneath I've put *If you don't like something, eat it.*

Izzie looks confused. "What does that even mean?"

"I don't know – I just thought it sounded good. What else am I supposed to say? Hannah, words of wisdom?"

She looks thoughtful. "In novels, injustice is punished and the righteous flourish. After a while, and after a fair bit of suffering. But then again, sometimes the righteous just die and go to heaven. That's their reward."

"But I'm not righteous and I want to flourish now without any suffering! And I have no intention of dying," I say.

"Sorry," Hannah says. "Strangely enough, Jane Austen doesn't always have wise words to say on how to survive in a multi-media world . . ."

Great – no help from the witch *or* the bookworm.

At this moment, there is a knock on the door. The inside door, not the outside one that everyone uses. No one uses the inside door except Hannah and she's sat here with us. Hannah's family never come down – that's why we like it here.

We look at each other. Hannah yells, "Come in!"

Through the door comes Hannah's brother Alex and, with him – pinch yourselves cos it's true – Matt Paige. Yes, *that* Matt Paige, the one I have a huge and secret crush on, the Matt Paige who's in my head every night as I go to sleep – the one I've been on numerous dates with, the one I've kissed, got married to and had three children with (all girls, if you're interested).

"Hi," says Alex.

"Hi," says Matt.

"Hi," I say, trying to look cool, but suddenly I'm aware that I'm running a temperature of forty degrees and my heart has decided to do a drum and bass rhythm with a dub-step vibe.

FFS, he's just a boy.

But he is lovely. If I could, I'd just lie down at his feet and tell him I love him.

Did I actually think that? Have I just broken every rule I hold dear, for a BOY?

So I pull myself together – I will not be so pathetic! I smile a bit, to look friendly, but not enough to show how much I like him. I think I end up grimacing like a constipated parrot.

"So, Jess," Alex says, "what exactly have you been up to?"

I've known Alex since I was six. He's sort of skinny and a bit ginger. Whereas Hannah looks like some kind of artist's model, Alex looks like a slightly more attractive Ron Weasley. One good thing about this is that I think I can speak to him without my voice wavering several octaves.

"Oh, you know, the usual. Registration, two altercations with Zara Lovechild, getting into a confrontation with a teacher," I say. "Oh yes, and becoming a YouTube hit. No sweat."

"So it *was* you," Matt says. "Now I see."

What does he mean by that? I will have to analyse every possible different interpretation later – I don't have time now. I'm too busy hanging on his every word.

"What happened?" Matt asks, fixing me with his dark brown eyes, his hair falling down over them. So I tell him, and just manage to stop myself from sweeping his hair back from his forehead.

"Zara is such a cow," Alex says with surprising anger.

I look at him, taken aback.

"I mean, you're not fat," he says. "She's just too skinny."

"Cheers, mate," I say. "I'll make you some of your favourite brownies if you like."

"So you're a good cook then?" Matt says.

"The best!" Alex says with pride. "She should be on TV. Have you seen this?" He pulls out his phone and shows Matt a photo of my gingerbread school.

"Cool," Matt says. "You did that?"

"I was bored," I say and blush.

"Look at the detail," says Izzie.

"Yeah, I see it," he says and smiles at me.

I allow myself a small smile back.

"So you're Cat Jones's little sister then?" he continues.

I wait for a second for him to make some comment about not believing that we're sisters or that I'm not in fact that little at all. He doesn't do either. SCORE!

"You can tell by your eyes." He noticed my EYES (and I think that they are quite nice actually – people often tell me I have nice eyes).

"She's going out with Jack Armstrong from your school," I drop in.

Alex and Matt exchange glances.

"What?" says Izzie. "Is he up to something?"

Matt shrugs. "No . . . He does seem to hang out with his ex a lot. But then that's not a crime."

Alex changes the subject. "Good work there, Jones, you did well with Zara and Brown, but Brown is gonna want to put your head on a spike. Come on, Matt, we need to practise. The band's waiting."

"Oh, I didn't know you guys were in a band," I find myself saying. "What kind of music are you into?"

Alex answers, "You know, Jones, you could come and listen to us rehearse if you like."

I'm about to jump up and follow them out of the door, but I find a firm hand on my arm and a voice saying, "Thanks, but we've got stuff to do."

The tone of Hannah's voice means that I mustn't argue back, for reasons I don't understand.

The guys start to go, but Matt stops in the doorway and turns back. "I'm having a few guys over two weeks on Saturday, parents are out. You wanna come?" He smiles and takes us all in: the fat girl, the bookworm and the witch. "All of you."

"Great," I croak. "We'll check our diaries."

The door shuts.

I recline on the non-reclining recliner. My heart really is going to pop this time. I want to be independent, mature, follow my own path. But then the second this guy, this one guy talks to me, it's like I'm going to explode.

Izzie mutters, "Not sure that I want to go."

Hannah stares at her. "Well, *you* might not want to but a certain somebody does!"

Izzie's head docs a tennis swivel from me to Hannah. "What, have I just missed something?"

"Only the most enormous amount of sexual tension," Hannah says.

Izzie looks closely at me. "You fancy *Alex*?" Her voice goes all strange and wavery at the end.

I spit out my hot chocolate. "No," I say.

"Okay, keep your hair on," she says. "Well, that leaves Matt."

"Yes," says Hannah, "it does."

And they both look at me.

My secret crush is now a not-so-secret crush.

Chapter 9

Invisible Rule № 6: In this enlightened age, girls are still not allowed to ask guys out. You have to wait for them to make a move. Otherwise you're "pushy". Or "easy". Either way, it's not very ladylike.

I sigh. I've kept this madness locked up inside me for too long. "I just think he seems nice."

"Nice" seems a very bland word for all the emotions that swept through me a few minutes ago. I mean, my heart is only just returning to a normal beat. In fact, I'm not even sure that my heart is still inside me. I think it's following Matt up the stairs into the house, squealing, "Love me, love me, do whatever you want with me."

I try to pull myself together.

Hannah and Izzie keep looking at me with open mouths.

"Hannah, surely you realised before – I asked you all those questions about him."

Hannah shakes her head. I really don't like this silence. I take a deep breath. I mean, we do talk about boys all the time. Which ones are okay, which ones are not. But it is a bit of a touchy subject as Hannah was going out with Lucas Harrison for three months until he really started giving her grief for not sleeping with him.

So she did.

And then he dumped her anyway.

Ouch. So you know, it's easier sometimes just to ask her about what she's reading. I mean, guys in Jane Austen books just don't do that.

And Izzie. Well, TBH, she lives in a different area to us and still hangs out with guys she went to primary school with. She doesn't really talk much about them but she does get lots of text messages that she won't share with us and then disappears for no reason. So either she has other "friends" or she's some kind of superwitch who turns into a crime fighter when things get rough on her estate. We could be a crime fighting duo – Superwitch and Fat Girl.

And then there's me. I've kissed and been kissed. I mean, I go to parties. At the end of the evening, you can normally find someone who's not paired off and is happy to snog (and the rest) for a while. Dom and I had a thing for a bit where we tried stuff out on each other. But I've not really had a boyfriend. Not a proper public one. And believe it or not, I think I could have. A few boys have really seemed to like me. But I never liked them enough to go beyond friends. I don't know if it's Gran's influence or too many silly rom-coms. I just want to go out with someone who makes me feel amazing.

And now I've set my heart on one of the hottest guys around. Because when he actually looks at me, it is the most amazing feeling I've ever had.

Sigh.

"Is he unbelievably out of my league?"

They look long and hard at each other.

Ouch. These are good friends. They are thinking very quickly how to let me down kindly. I love them both for this.

Hannah starts slowly. "His last girlfriend was . . . a bit different from you."

I nod, this could be helpful, I don't know all of this. "So, two things. A – is he single? And B – how was she different?"

And Hannah takes her time on this one. "She was . . . high maintenance."

What does that even mean?

"You mean she was difficult, or she took great care of herself?"

Izzie chips in here. "I saw them in Starbucks sometimes. She ordered extra hot, skinny macchiato, easy on the syrup. And then she only drank half. I'd say both."

Taking a deep breath, I have to say this and I have to hear their answer. "So she's prettier than me, thinner than me and better dressed than me. And knows when to stop eating."

Izzie and Hannah shrug.

"Maybe, depends on your opinion," says Hannah.

"That's no answer," I say. "She is or she isn't."

Hannah tells me the truth. "Yes, she's thinner than you. But, Jess, you've always said you don't care about that. You're pretty, she's pretty. You don't care about fashion really, and she does."

"I know what I've said," I say. "But I do care about clothes. I just find them difficult. I mean, shop girls give me the evil eye every time I walk in, and *you* want to try having to get to the back of the clothes rack every time, because they put all the smaller sizes at the front!"

Hannah moves towards the little hob. "Time for more hot chocolates, I think."

Oh dear. Things are that bad then.

We drink our hot chocolates but for once my heart just isn't in it.

I think they sense I'm in a bad place and so, as I slug the drink back, they pass the time on the laptop, calling out to me when they think something will amuse me. But I need to go. I need to be on my own for a bit.

"I'm off," I mutter. "Back home, to think this all through. It's been one helluva day."

My lovely friends smile back at me. "Yes," they agree.

Hannah says, "I'll ring later."

I nod and dodge out through the door.

Unusually for me, I just don't know what to do with myself. I wander to the patch of lawn on the way from Hannah's house to mine. I sit on the grass and look up at the trees for a bit. They wobble, in rather a nice way, in the wind. The afternoon is late and warm. My phone constantly buzzes now I've turned it on but I ignore it. I just don't think that anyone is going to have anything to say that I actually want to hear today.

As I sit there, guess who walks past, presumably going back home to his house round the corner? Yes, it's Mr Wonderful himself.

He sort of slouches along, with his shoulders bunched, as if to walk at his full height might give him an unfair advantage over the world. I sigh. Do I call him over?

"Hey!" Apparently yes, I do. My current self seems to think that this would be a good idea. My current self has not thought to check my appearance or consider what on earth I'm going to say.

Anyway, Matt sees me, smiles what appears to be a genuine smile, crosses the road and throws himself down next to me on the grass. He's sitting right beside me. Maybe seventeen centimetres apart? Does that mean he likes me? Or does that mean he's keeping his distance? My brain cannot cope with these mathematical and emotional calculations!

"How did the practice go?" I ask.

"Okay," he says. "Alex's got homework so we had to finish. But we've got a gig coming up. And in fact we've just been booked to play at your Prom. Your pal Zara organised it."

"Great," I say. But while I love the idea of him being at the Prom, I can't help but think that Zara had other reasons than just the excellence of the band when she booked them.

And then there's a silence. I don't want a silence, I'm scared of silence. Silence means we're not compatible. Him walking away from me is the scariest thing in the world right now.

We both start to speak at the same time and then we both laugh.

"You first," I say.

"Oh, I was just going to say that if you do come to my party, then Zara will be there. I just want you to know."

"Ah – so that's why you invited me! I'm the entertainment. If things get dull, then you want me to pick another fight with Zara?" Wow. That was quite clever. Especially given it's a huge challenge to get a syllable out without quivering with emotion.

"Great idea. Female mud-wrestling – yeah, that would be great. Very post-modern."

He's clearly more intelligent than me. But I don't want to show him I don't know what post-modern means, so I just laugh. I think I might have just tossed my hair too, to distract from my lack of knowledge. I'll Google it later.

"Well, if it's wrestling, she doesn't stand a chance. I'll break her like a twig."

He makes a face. "Don't be too tough on her. Have you ever met her mother? She can be a bit intense."

I stare at him. "If we're gonna compare weird families, then mine win!" I tell him about Gran, about Lauren and her invisible friend, the fact that Dad thinks he's still living in the nineties and Mum's general uptightness about everything.

"Okay, okay," he smiles, "you have it tough too. But what I'm trying to say is that Zara isn't all bad. She can be funny."

I sniff. "Maybe if you're a boy. I don't think she shows that side at school."

"True," he agrees. "You know, she's probably just a bit intimidated by you."

"Me?" I protest. "I love kittens and bunnies and all things cute. I'm not intimidating!"

"Yeah, right," he says. "I've only just met you, but there's something about you. You're clearly never short of anything to say. You're a bit different to other girls. You're cool, Jess Jones."

And there you are. The best moment of my life so far. Granny would be ashamed of me, but I don't care. He looked in my eyes, and said I was cool.

Just as I'm mulling over something clever to say, he leaps to his feet.

"Gotta go, Jess. History essay calls. But give me your number." He stabs it into his phone and slouches off into the distance.

I may actually be the happiest girl in the entire universe.

He's got my number.

But will he ever use it?

Chapter 10

Invisible Rule № 7: Life is generally easier if you conform. But it is also duller. And you have to sell your soul a bit at the same time.

My house is on the other side of the street. I sigh. Can I get in and up to my room without being spotted? I could be ambushed by Dad for one of his little chats, or Mum might have a second go at me. I can't imagine what Cat's reaction will be.

But I'm not really thinking about Cat. I'm thinking about Matt. Oh, it rhymes!

Pull yourself together, Jess, I tell myself. Here's the deal. There are so many rules about boys and boyfriends that my brain just hurts even thinking about them, but here are some:

1. Having a boyfriend makes you cool. Cos it's like there's at least one person in the world who is prepared to stand up in public and say "This girl is hot. I like this girl. I am not ashamed to be seen with her."
2. Having a fit boyfriend makes you even cooler.
3. Bonus points if he doesn't have (many) spots and smells nice.
4. Bonus points if he is taller than you.
5. Triple bonus points if he's rich and goes to the posh school down the road.
6. Zillion points if he's actually a decent human being and treats you remotely nicely i.e. not lying about stuff you do in private and then putting it all over Facebook and making you look bad.

If I do get Matt to like me, he would definitely meet the first five. And I think he's also 6. He just looks like a good guy. I know I'm biased, but he just does. Surely my hormones wouldn't be so cruel as to make me go crazy for some crappy arrogant crap head?

Who knows what hormones do to us? Maybe love is just one great big hormone rush . . .

I think about this as I walk home.

Irony alert. Guess who's sitting in my kitchen, big sweating hands pawing over my sister. Yep, it's Jack, the all-important BOYFRIEND. Problem is that IMHO he's an A* asshat.

Picture the scene. Cat slouches, unsmiling (i.e. in Cat default position) at the table, Jack sits next to her, his arm around her, slowly stroking her arm with small possessive movements, but his eyes are welded on my mum's bum as she bends over, getting something out of the oven. I stand in the doorway for a second, swaying ever so slightly. In theory, Jack fits all the criteria for a boyfriend, except of course I need to add in a rule against checking out the intimate body areas of female family members. (Okay I'm not one to discriminate – male family members too. Yep, if your boyfriend looks at your dad's privates, then we all know that everyone's on to a loser here!!)

Jack's eyes flicker over to me. He knows that I've seen him staring at Mum's bum but he doesn't look embarrassed – he seems to think it's all very funny. Cat appears oblivious to anything. Will she ever speak again? I suppose I don't really want to know the answer to this but what do each of them get out of this relationship? I suppose they look good together, like some kind of god-awful perfume advert. But he gives me the creeps. He stares at me, looks me up and down, eyes staying on the boobs just a bit too long. I wish he would drop dead. I mean, when Dom looks at my boobs, that's one thing. But this – this is something else.

As Mum struggles with the weight of the tray she's pulling out the oven, Jack leaps up to help her.

"Let me help," he purrs as he takes it from her and puts it safely on to the table. "Smells delicious," he says and then, with a smile and a pause, "Just like you, Mrs Jones."

Mum blushes and hits him with a tea towel, Jack smirks and Cat looks blank. I think that I'm going to hurl in the kitchen bin.

"Call me Annabel, please Jack. You make me feel so old," Mum says.

Finally Mum sees me. For a moment, I think there's going to be rerun of this morning. But clearly she doesn't want a row in front of Jack, so she fixes a blank smile on her face. "Oh darling," she says, "I was wondering where you were."

I stare at her. "Where do you think I was?" I say. "I was at Hannah's, where I always am."

She holds my gaze for a moment. "You are welcome to have your friends round here, you know."

I shrug. "More privacy there."

She bridles. "Well, I've done some chicken for tea. There's salad on the table. Dad's gone out so it's just the four of us." She turns on a mega-watt smile for Jack, who smiles back.

"I'll be Daddy then, shall I?" He winks.

I may have to either kill myself or gouge his eyes out with a paring knife. Is it just me? Is this just cute boyfriend behaviour, or is this just a bit weird? Cat is now intent on her phone. Something she reads makes her eyes narrow just for a second.

Jack reaches over and without a word takes the phone from her hand and turns it off.

WTF? You don't mess with someone's phone. That's just weird. I watch Cat to see if she'll actually do anything. Cat looks at him. He smiles back. If it were me, I'd smack him.

I look to Mum to see if she's picking up on his passive aggressive tendencies, but she just smiles again. "Good idea, Jack. Nice to have you with us, Cat."

My beautiful sister is as silent and impassive as ever. But she reaches over Jack, takes back her phone, switches it on and puts it carefully back on the table next to her. I smile, Jack laughs, but there is no warmth in his eyes. *Cat–1, Idiot Boyfriend–0.*

As Mum dishes out the chicken breast on to plates, I look critically at her work. "They're more tender if you cook them with the skin on," I start.

"Too many calories," Mum says bluntly. "Have some salad."

"Looks lovely, Annabel. I'm partial to a bit of tender breast myself," Jack says.

See? The boy's an ASSHAT.

Mum giggles, Cat is silent. I wish Dad were here.

I look round for the salad dressing but can't see any so I walk over to the larder to get the oil, vinegar and mustard. As I whip them up, I watch my mum and sister at work on the table.

Mum piles a huge amount of rocket and tomato next to her chicken. Carefully, she goes through the leaves and returns every single olive back into the salad bowl. FML, what's the point of making a salad with olives if you're going to take them all out again?

Cat regards her chicken carefully. Cuts it in half. And then in half again. Puts three quarters of it back and then cuts the remainder into tiny baby-sized mouthfuls. She very deliberately begins to chew each mouthful twenty times and drinks between each mouthful. Yes, Cat eats like she's a celebrity.

I return to the table with my freshly made and particularly well-seasoned dressing. I've added a bit of fresh tarragon to bring out the flavour of the chicken and the tomato. After pouring it liberally over my meal, I offer the jug to Mum and Cat. Both wave it away but I see Mum's hand occasionally edge towards it. I bite into the salad and savour the rich taste of the dressing. "Um," is all I can manage, "you don't know what you're missing."

"Better go easy on that, Jess," Jack says. "Didn't I hear that you had some kind of wardrobe malfunction at school today?" He smiles at me like a shark. Mum titters and Cat remains quiet.

"Are you calling me fat?" I return, deciding to go for direct confrontation tonight. And depending on his answer I have more ammunition up my sleeves.

"Jess," Mum reprimands me, "don't be so sensitive."

Jack goes into super smooth mode. "Course not, Jess. Curves are all the rage, right? You're just so bootilicious," he says, "and, how else can I put it – pleasantly plump?"

I stare at him, words and emotions pounding round inside my head but somehow not making it as far as my mouth. *C'mon, Jess, say something good.* I need a moment to think this through and, while doing so, I enjoy my chicken. Never start a verbal assault with a full mouth of food.

We all eat in silence.

"I was talking to Matt and Alex today, Jack," I say.

"Fascinating," Jack says coldly.

I choose my words carefully. I don't want to say anything to upset Cat but I do want Jack to know that I know stuff.

"They said you hang out with them sometimes. They told me who else you hang out with too."

My words hang in the air. Have I said too much or not enough?

Jack glares at me, Cat stares at me. The two of them then exchange a glance. Cat's eyes are full of anger. Did she pick up on what I meant? I thought I was being subtle . . .

Awks. Cat stops, with most of her small portion of food still left to go. "Thanks, Mum," she says, and pushes her food away. Jack pushes her plate towards me. "Want to finish off my seconds?" he says with a glint in his eyes.

"Not my style," I return. Actually, normally I would eat it. But not in front of him.

I'd like to think that that's *Jess–1, Asshat–0*.

But somehow I'm just not that sure any more.

Chapter 11

Jess Observation № 4: The internet is great for cheating on your homework (sorry, for independent research) but it's also just another way to fail at life.

I can't spend any more time with people who all clearly find me less than satisfactory in some kind of way.

If you had a car boot sale for family members, Mum and Cat would be in the front of the queue, clamouring to get rid of me and exchange me for some kind of skinny plastic robot girl who only says "OMG", "Your shoes are FABULOUS!" and "I'm so fat, I need to lose ten pounds."

I head up to my room to try and sort out the mess of feelings that are swirling around inside me like some kind of psychedelic kaleidoscope. Maybe I should try one of Gran's "herbal" cigarettes.

Today has officially been the weirdest of my life. It felt cool to get one over on Zara. It felt great to walk away from Mrs Brown. That was amazing and possibly my finest few seconds on this planet to date. In my head, I'm a lot cooler and braver than I am in real life. For a few seconds, I was the person that I wanted to be – no compromise, no regrets.

Even better and weirder – those cool moments are now on the internet and people might be watching all over the world. (Downer that they'll see my legs but let's just gloss over that for now.)

And then the highest high –

Matt Paige has:

1. Found out who I am.
2. Looked straight in my eyes and not laughed or puked.
3. Asked me to his party.
4. Asked for my number.

This is all amazingly amazing. In fact, it's all tickety-boo.

So why am I now feeling so low? Is it that fantasy guys are so much better when they're fantasy? Fantasy guys only say what I want them to say, they only do what I want them to do. Matt is my fantasy guy but now reality and fantasy are going to collide and I just don't think it will end well.

But I want it to.

I want my fantasy. I want him to like me, to laugh at my jokes, to brush the hair from my eyes, look deeply into my eyes again, then kiss me. I want it to be real and I still want it to be perfect.

But I'm not perfect. So it's not going to happen.

When it's just me and boys in general, I'm fine about the way I look. I'm not skinny, I'm not a whale, I'm just a bit bigger than most of the girls in my year. I'm not the biggest. And that's okay because it's me and I'm happy about the way I look. Aren't I?

But why did my heart sink when I saw me on the clip? Because I didn't think I was as fat as that? Because all the girls around me were obviously thinner?

I look at the clip again. There I am, looking like me. And there are all the other girls, looking generally thin, all cheering me on.

The truth is I'd LIKE to be happy about the way I look cos it's my way of not being superficial. I want to think that people like me for me. Not because I fit some weird idea of what being pretty is that involves not eating and looking ill.

It's like you have to choose between life and beauty.

But you only get a really good life if you're beautiful.

And to be beautiful you have to conform.

And I don't want to conform.

But I do want Matt Paige to kiss me.

And part of me feels sick about how out of control I felt when he looked at me. Part of me was overwhelmed and excited. Another part of me, a piece of ice in my brain, was thinking, *He's just a boy, why are you reacting like this?* But I didn't have a choice, my heart just went mad and I nearly died from excitement. From him just looking at me.

Imagine, what would happen if he did kiss me?

I'd spontaneously combust in flames with pleasure. But that's not such a bad way to go.

Jeez, this is confusing. I think I've got two choices:

1. Just go to the party. Be me. Fat Jess. And see if he really does like me.
2. Turn myself into the kind of girl who gets kissed at parties. And not just at the end of the evening when some boy, out of his mind of vodka, stumbles on to you and decides that the fat girl will do.

I've got two and a half weeks.

I could make myself thinner in that time.

I could take control of my destiny and get my man.

A bit of me reminds myself that it's the Twenty-first Century – and I'm thinking about starving myself to get a boyfriend? Have I watched just one too many rom-coms?

Or am I just sixteen and having a really intense crush and prepared to do anything to make it happen?

I wish I was older and then I'd know the answer to these questions.

Then I notice something in my room that wasn't there before.

In the corner of my room, draped over the chair, is a long parcel. The colour of the wrapping makes me think that it's from one of the few shops who design clothes that I really like. Mum said she'd bought me a dress. This must be it.

Maybe it's a peace offering.

I rip off the covering and take out the dress.

It's perfect.

I put it up to my face – the colour, soft pink, is exquisite. It's low cut enough to suggest my boobs without being blatant, shaped for curves, still good over jeans or leggings – sexy but cool. I have to give it to her. My mum does know something about fashion.

I love the dress; I hope it loves me.

Then a thought strikes me.

I check the label.

I feel like being sick.

The cow.

It's one size too small for me. The shop does stock my size

but she decided to get me one size too small. Because I'm no good to her like I am.

I strip down to bra and pants and put it on.

The dress may be perfect but I am not.

I look at myself in the mirror.

In the mirror, a fat girl stands, her eyes holes of misery in her face. Her boobs stretch the fabric, her stomach looks enormous, and the material shines over her bum.

I imagine what Mum would say if she was here. *"If you'd just put a bit of effort in, in a few weeks, you'd look a million dollars."*

I would like to look a million dollars. I would like to look in a mirror and be happy.

But would I still be me?

The dress says, "Just try for a few days and see how it goes."

The dress says, "No pressure, no compromise."

The dress says, "Find nice food that is lower in calories. Look at the saturated fat content. Hell, would it kill you to do some exercise?"

The dress says, "Just give it two weeks."

How many corny movies have I seen where the geeky girl is transformed into some kind of goddess and then gets the guy? He looks at her in a new way, like boys look at Cat, like Matt looked at me once.

And that could be me.

I want it to be me.

I make my way down to the kitchen with an empty feeling inside me. It's all dark and quiet. The kitchen is in shadow and when I open the fridge, butter yellow light falls across the black tiles. I don't really need to look inside cos I know every item in there.

I take out the box of cupcakes left over from this morning.

I eat one.

I put my hand out for one more, but though I'd like to eat it, I'm just too full. If I eat it, I'll burst. Mum and Dad may come down for breakfast tomorrow and find me spread thinly across the tiled floor.

I like to think that Lauren would miss me.

I smell its light sponge, give it a little kiss and then put it back.

Time for a new, different Jess. A thinner Jess.

That's got to be good, right?

Chapter 12

Invisible Rule № 8: Guys can't wear pink. Or wear skirts. Or glitter. Which makes some of them sad, I think. Pink's just a colour, isn't it?

I didn't sleep well last night.
Here are just a few reasons.
1. I ate enough food to solve several food shortages in LEDC last night (guess who's sitting her Geography exam soon?).
2. I have a meeting with the head and my parents this morning.
3. Matt Paige looked at me.
4. I need to think of a way to get my own back on Zara.
5. I, Jesobel Jones, have decided to go on a diet even though I have always laughed at those who do. I have sold out. I no longer have any reason to exist. I may just disappear at any time.

And now I'm awake and I don't see much chance of going back to sleep, given the incredibly loud noise from outside. Bloody birds. It's early spring and all they can do at five a.m. is tweet. Don't they have mobiles for that? Mother Nature needs to catch up PDQ and get them on the real Twitter and Western Europe will sleep a lot better. (Am I making any sense? Clearly the idea of being on a diet has tipped me over the edge.)

So, I think, this is my first day of dieting. So far, so good. I've been awake for ten minutes and I've not eaten anything. Way to go me.

I think over my general understanding of dieting.
1. I need to burn more calories than I eat.
2. So less is good. The less I eat, the more I'll lose.

(Some disagree on this but I don't see how you can eat lots of food and still lose weight. There are, however, lots of things in the world that I don't understand: the Higgs-Boson particle, patterned leggings, why anyone watches reality TV . . .) Celebrities seem to go on weird diets where they eat nothing but cabbage or maple syrup. The last one seems to make more sense but the first one sounds like a disaster. Okay, you might be skinny but your farts would kill off any living organisms standing next to you. Skinny but lonely would be the end result and what's the use of that?

3. Fruit and veg are best, I think, but beyond that it gets all confusing. Good carbs, bad carbs, good fats, bad fats . . . weird diets with even weirder names. I could spend a lifetime on Google researching this but I think I'll just stick with Rule Number 1.

So here I am, on zero calories but with a full stomach. If I do some exercise, then I'll be in minus calories and then I can eat something (salady) later in the day. This seems like a good idea. I'm too wired to sleep and the streets should be quite quiet at this hour of the morning. Mum won't be too stoked to find me running around the neighbourhood on my own but then surely all would be forgiven when she finds out why. And after all, I've got my mobile phone – my adult to child tracker device – so what can possibly go wrong?

So what to wear? Never my strong point. Obvs the main idea is sweats and trainers – even I can work that out. But it's the underwear that's troubling me. I swim, I go to the gym sometimes, but I've never actually run any distance. And the main reason for that is my boobs.

Apparently, constructing a bra is one of the most difficult engineering tasks known to humankind. You have to make a structure that's comfortable to wear and that can accommodate two unsupported blobs of jelly that can move up, down, sideways and any variation in between. I rummage through my drawers to see what I can do about this. Oh, yes, and be vaguely attractive – i.e. not something Gran would wear. Actually Gran doesn't bother with a bra any more. Which is a bit scary. But then she's mildly stoned most of the time so I suppose she doesn't care.

Fortunately, whatever failings my mum has, she is very fussy about my bras and so, as I pull out one elastic garment after the other, I find that I am the proud owner of three sports bras. Well, I think, three should do the trick.

So without any further mucking about, I put them on. All three. I jump up and down gently just to demonstrate. Solid as a rock. Not a wibble, not a wobble. Two large boobs, firmly strapped in place. After pulling on an old hoodie and trackies, I look at myself in the mirror. Something peculiar has happened to my boobs. They now appear to have been relocated just beneath each ear. A fit of giggles threatens to consume me. I force them down (the giggles, not the boobs – they're staying exactly there). No time for humour, Jess, I tell myself. Exercise is serious business.

I squeak down the stairs. There are snuffles from various bedrooms but no one leaps out at me and asks what I'm doing. Within seconds, I've unlocked the front door, carefully pushed it back, waited for a few seconds so Mum can come rushing down to demand what I'm up to.

Nothing. I've made it outside.

I'm vaguely disappointed.

Now what?

Apart from the birds, there's not much going on. No one on the streets, very few lights on in dark houses, a solitary car slowly going past. Over the dark roofs, the pale blue sky is streaked with wisps of pink gold. Look at me – no breakfast is making me all poetic. I'll be writing sonnets and turning into an emo before you know what's happening. Shaking off such ideas, I take a deep breath, open the front gate and then put one foot in front of the other. That's running, isn't it? I repeat the process, only more quickly this time, and off I go.

Okay, I'm doing okay – I've reached the end of the road and I've not died. The air feels harsh in my lungs and I'm getting hotter but apart from that I'm okay, honestly. Boobs are staying where they should be, feet don't hurt. Lungs are doing okay and I do a bit of Biology revision, picturing in my head a multicolour dissection of my lungs with blue and red

THE LIVES AND LOVES OF JESOBEL JONES

lines to show oxygenated blood going out and deoxygenated blood coming in. Sorted – the A* will be mine! By now, end of the next road, my breath is coming thick and fast and my chest is starting to hurt. I head towards the park – I can do a few laps there and then think about heading for home. Half an hour – steady pace – no food until lunchtime – easy peasy lemon squeezy.

In the distance, I see two figures running towards me on the opposite pavement. All of a sudden, I think about who they might be. There's a strong possibility that they are SOWs, that they'll know my mum and tell her all about my early morning running.

I suppose it doesn't matter if anyone sees me but just at the moment I want everything to be secret, so I pull my hood over my face and continue. Truth is, would anyone recognise me now anyway? Surely my face has now swollen up into some alien-like mask that bears little resemblance to me and more to something jumping out at you in the dark in some gory space film.

The two skinny figures get closer and the slightly smaller one, though running at pace, is still managing to talk at great length, volume and speed. It's a voice that I recognise, having a peculiarly nasal quality and piercing tone. They're only feet from me, they don't seem to have noticed me but I'll bet you a brioche that it's Zara Lovechild.

For a second, heat blazes through my mind, confusing my thought processes. They run nearer me, I slowly come nearer to them. Any second now, Zara will see me and then she'll know she's got me. She will know that I have caved in.

A space opens out on my left. There's a low hedge that backs on to the bowling green. Panic takes over me. I just don't want her to see me.

I jump over the hedge and fall flat on my back. I hold my breath. I hear Zara's voice whinge on about how much revision she's done. Her voice is over my head, she just needs to look down and there I'll be: laid out at her tiny feet like some kind of a sacrifice at the plastic altar of meanness.

"Zara, darling, Chloe Simcock's daughter got eleven A stars so I don't see why you can't," I hear the other person say. I wonder if this is the she-wolf mother that Matt talked about.

"Mummy, I can't – that's just unfair."

"Eleven A stars and you can have the nose job. That's the deal."

They're over me, past me and then they run on, Zara's voice slowly disappearing until she's just an annoying mosquito in the distance.

Nose job? In return for A*s? Even for round here, home of the WAG, that's a bit messed up.

Speaking of which, I then begin to wonder if I've jumped into some dog poo

There's no doubt about the score now.

Skinny People–1, Jess–0.

Chapter 13

Invisible Rule № 9: Only girls are told to be nice – boys never are. Niceness is pretty much a girl thing. Niceness sucks.

I'm not feeling the best, TBH, as I trudge to the house. On the plus side, thanks to the three sports bras, I've done some exercise without causing any collateral damage to passers-by or myself with my out-of-control boobs. And let me tell you, nothing feels as good as taking three bras off. I now begin to think that I understand what those poor Victorian girls must have felt like in corsets. There's this moment of joy when all that strapped down flesh makes a bid for freedom.

Another plus – I have not eaten anything. On the negative side, I jumped over a wall to avoid being seen by a fellow pupil and threw myself to the ground without thinking about what lay there. Again, it's clearly a good day for Scorpios (though I don't believe in that BS) cos it was a dog-dirt free zone. I think I've used up a bit of today's luck (don't believe in luck either – God, I'm confused). And it's only 6.33. Today's gonna be a long one.

I'm beginning to get a bit hungry but I need to avoid food if I'm going to get into that bloody dress. So no breakfast for Jess. Black coffee, or green tea. Only a few calories there.

I peer round the living-room door. Lauren is watching *Buffy the Vampire Slayer* with an empty cushion next to her, clearly showing Alice's presence. It's Alice's favourite TV show but Lauren gets nightmares from it. Not being the responsible adult around here, I leave her to it.

Mum will be having her normal fruit salad with a sprinkling of muesli for breakfast. Someday, she'll have two pieces of pineapple. Woo hoo. How to live on the edge!

She looks sad. It's not a pineapple day, poor Mum. She seems put out as she rummages through all the cereal boxes.

"Jess, have you seen my muesli – you know, the really expensive stuff in the purple box? From Waitrose?" (Mum mostly shops at Aldi but she puts everything into Waitrose bags so as to kid the neighbours.)

I shake my head as I aim for the cappuccino machine. Double espresso for me – keep me going for a while.

"Have you seen Mummy's special cereal in the purple box?" Mum asks as Lauren comes into the kitchen.

Lauren puts her head on one side and puts her finger to her cheek. She's been watching too much TV on how to be a cute child.

"The purple box?" she repeats.

"Yes," says Mum.

"With the picture of the birdies on?" says Lauren.

"Yes," says Mum.

"The cereal that looks like sawdust with rabbit poo in it?" Lauren says. (She might be four, but she's right.)

"Yes, that's one way of looking at it."

Lauren pauses. "It's in the rabbit hutch."

Mum attempts to control her face and fails. "And why would it be in the rabbit hutch?"

My little sister is deep in thought again. "I put it there."

Mum takes a long breath. "And why might you do that?"

"Cos we'd run out of sawdust and you told me to clean the hutch."

I can tell Mum is trying very hard to be mindful but then she just gives up.

"LAUREN, THAT WAS NOT SAWDUST – THAT WAS VERY EXPENSIVE FOOD."

"Alice told me to!" Lauren begins to howl.

No one notices me as I take my coffee and retreat to my room. It's more peaceful in there. I sip my coffee as I check my various accounts on my phone – FB, Twitter, you name it. Still lots of messages, all going on about yesterday.

And there's a new clip. Someone has re-edited a longer version and put it to music.

Wow. Then I scroll down to the comments. Ouch. Some good, some bad. Now I know how the whole world sees me. And that's fat.

I mean, we all know that the internet is a cruel world, transforming generally polite people into trolls who foam at the mouth and will say anything, actually *anything*, in order to get someone to pay them some attention.

So the comments range from, *This girl is cool, I like her* to *If I looked like this girl, I'd kill myself.* Nice. This being on the internet thing might require a thicker skin than I have.

Then my brain starts to hurt so I give up and relive (I've only done this two hundred times already) what Matt said to me and how he smiled. My whole body tingles just at the memory.

Before you know it, it's time to go to school.

Nine o'clock meeting with Mr Ambrose.

FML.

So there we are – me, Dad and Mum. Waiting to meet the Headmaster. Joy.

We wait in the rather shabby entrance to the school, me in my school uniform that makes me look like I've just stepped out of an Enid Blyton book, Mum who looks amazing and Dad who looks like he's just come back from an all-nighter somewhere, hiding behind his shades.

"Stephen," Mum hisses as she readjusts her stilettoes and repositions her cleavage, "take those bloody things off. You look ridiculous."

He grunts, "'S too early, 's too bright," and slumps down further into the sofa. I'm sorta proud of him. Okay, he's not the most responsible father in the world but perhaps I'm a bit like him in a strange sort of way. He doesn't really live by many rules that I can see, so maybe that's where I get it from. Sometimes you can just about tell that he's his mother's son. Yep, Stephen and Gran, it's all your fault. I don't tell him this just now; he looks sad enough as it is.

Various teachers walk past, chatting, and give us a bit of a stare. I suppose that they must have been talking about me too. Do they think I'm a bully or not?

Just after 9.05, we're shown to the office. No need to knock; we go straight in. I feel like some kind of celebrity. That feeling soon goes away.

Inside the rather dull and stuffy office sits Mr Ambrose, the Head of our school, who is also rather dull and stuffy. Behind him is a rather gruesome crucifix with Our Lord painfully impaled upon it. I've got nothing against Jesus. In fact, I think he's rather cool. I don't think he would have minded my lack of skirt. He might even have thought it all funny.

Mr Ambrose, on the other hand, is a very different kind of guy. He's a sort of grey man in a grey suit with grey eyes and a grey smile, if you know what I mean. I'm never quite sure how he ended up being the head of a girls' school, as he doesn't seem to like us very much. Despite his general greyness, his eyes do flicker for a second over Mum's rather low-cut top and her rather high-split skirt. There's a lot of flesh on show in this room and, for a change, it's not mine. OMG, maybe he thinks I did it on purpose after this, that I've learned my fashion sense from Mum. All of Mum's perfectly toned, tanned and cellulite-free thigh is now on show for all to see. Got to love her, she looks fab – but there's a time and a place and somehow I don't think this is either. It might be my imagination (let's put it down to the lack of food) but did Jesus's eyebrows just go up a notch just now, perhaps indicating general horror at my mother's lack of clothing?

Mum, however, thinks she's got this one sorted.

"Mr Ambrose," she purrs like she's working some sex line, "this has all been a terrible misunderstanding. We can put it straight in a few minutes, I'm sure, like sensible adults." Then she leans forward to make sure that he gets a good view of the boobs. To be fair, he doesn't know where to look, so he is a gentleman and just stares at me. I squirm. I'm not sure if Dad notices or whether he's so used to this sort of stuff he just doesn't care.

"Indeed, Mrs Jones," says Mr Ambrose.

She laughs her tinkly laugh. "Call me Annabel please, or Ms Hoylake if you must. We never married, you know."

So here I am with a mother who looks like a high-class pro and a father who looks (and is) a pot head and now she's telling Mr Ambrose they're not married. For a split second, I think I see something like sympathy in Mr Ambrose's grey eyes.

"Ms Hoylake, I need to talk to Jesobel first," he says as

firmly as a head teacher whose trousers are clearly suddenly too tight for him can.

"Jesobel," his steely eyes are now fixed on me, "you are accused of bullying a fellow pupil yesterday. We have evidence on camera. Then you were rude to a member of staff who attempted to discuss this with you and then you vacated the premises and took unauthorised absence for the rest of the day. Is that a fair summary of what happened?"

It's a good start from his point of view, cos technically everything he said is right. It's also just so very very wrong. I've been thinking all night how to put my side of the story and now's my chance and I can feel my words rolling away like marbles and I'm scrabbling to get them back.

"I wasn't bullying Zara," I say. "Earlier on, she pushed me. And then she came back for a second go. So I know what I said and did might look bad, but she was asking for it."

Mr Ambrose looks at me long and hard. "We don't have any evidence of that. She says you bullied her. And it's on camera. There's nothing to support your story."

I can feel Dad start to shuffle at this point. "Her *story*? You sound like you think she's making it up. My daughter tells the truth."

Go Dad! You almost sound like a dad, I think.

Mr Ambrose nods patronisingly in his direction, then turns back to me. "But what about what happened next? When you refused to do what a senior member of staff asked you to?"

"*The school depends on a relationship of mutual respect*," I say clearly. There's a pause.

"Yes?" he says, either with a question in his voice or he's unwittingly starting to sound like an Australian.

"That's from our mission statement," I say. (In case you don't know, a mission statement is some kind of waffly rubbish schools make up in case inspectors come in – they don't actually mean it.)

"And…" Mr Ambrose clearly has not got what I'm getting at yet.

"Mrs Brown," I say, "she broke that. She didn't treat me with any respect. She just called me a bully and said I was fat."

There is silence.

"You challenged the authority of a member of staff, Jesobel."

"She was rude to me; I was rude to her. We were both in the wrong."

"Yes, but you are the pupil. You know how we speak to teachers in this school."

"Yes, but she's the adult. She should be setting us a good example."

There is silence again.

"Jesobel, you need to apologise to the pupil concerned, and to Mrs Brown."

My voice quavers. "I'm sorry, sir, but I'm not going to do that. Unless they also apologise to me."

Dad rouses himself here. "Look, your old bat here, she was downright offensive. If I said what she said to Jess to another guy, he'd floor me. Jess was cool under the circs."

I'm not sure if Mr Ambrose understands any of this. He smiles his smooth smile. "I do understand your frustration. But we have evidence that Jesobel bullied another student. We have no evidence of earlier events. Jesobel does not have a track record of bullying so I might be persuaded to let that go."

He pauses for effect. "But schools are not democracies. The teacher's voice cannot be challenged and this must not go unpunished. Otherwise," he paused, "there would be chaos." He stops again. "I will not have disorder and chaos in my school. Therefore, Jesobel, you must apologise to Mrs Brown."

Gran was right. This is just a totalitarian regime of repression for teenagers.

There is more silence.

"There's the matter of your GCSEs, Jesobel. You are on course to do well. It would be such a pity if you were not allowed to sit your GCSEs, wouldn't it?" He smiles his cold smile. "All those years of work gone to waste because of a moment's pride on your part." He leans in now. "Our Lord – he had many things to say on pride. None of them good. On this occasion, Jesobel, I think you need to follow Our Lord's example and turn the other cheek."

I'm burning up here. He's saying that he knows I'm right but I just have to take it.

"You mean that you'd stop me sitting my GCSEs unless I apologise?" I say, my voice suddenly quavering.

"That is within my power, Jesobel."

Once he drops the GCSE bombshell, I can feel Mum squirming.

"I'm sure that Jess will be reasonable, won't you, darling?"

My words feel thick in my mouth. "And if I apologise, then there will be no other punishments?"

"Under the circumstances, I will overlook the unautho-rised absence, should your parents write a note explaining the medical reason behind it." He leans back and folds his fingers together, quite satisfied at the turn of events. "I think that will bring this unfortunate situation to an end."

My GCSEs. My route to A-levels, college, a way out of here. I've worked so hard for years for these. What choice do I have? If I'd eaten a good breakfast then I might be able to think of something, but currently I'm distracted by the fact that my stomach is growling and I've got coffee breath.

Dad is silent, Mum desperate, me full of hot tears of frus-tration.

I want them to protest, for Dad to leap up and say, "No, my daughter will not submit."

But he doesn't.

The room is full of the sound of capitulation (good word – look it up if you don't know what it means).

"So, Jesobel, you will write a letter of apology to both par-ties and you can return to lessons now. No letter – no school, no GCSEs."

I reach out for the paper he's pushed towards me, but in-side I am swearing revenge.

Then the final blow. "It has come to my attention that, un-fortunately, this event was filmed. Let me make it very clear that if you talk to anyone outside school about this event, then you can consider yourself immediately expelled. And, of course, you'll need to hand in your prefect's badge."

It's the small things that get to you sometimes.

Chapter 14

Invisible Rule № 10: The importance of subjects taught in school is directly opposite to their importance in the real world. All the Maths I'll ever need to know I can do on a calculator. A non-pro-grammable calculator.

I slouch back to class, seething with fury. The letter of apology is written. It sits on the desk of Mr Ambrose. It feels like it's got my soul trapped in it somehow. Okay, that's extreme, but they've got me trapped. I know they're wrong, they know they're wrong and yet . . . somehow he got me to write that bloody letter. All that sense of joy yesterday has suddenly been sucked from me. And I feel so empty. Literally and metaphorically.

Sighing, I make my way to the first lesson. Citizenship. All the things that grown-ups think children should know but are too embarrassed/scared to tell them themselves.

God/Jesus/whatever her name is, is clearly enjoying all of this, cos guess what the topic is? Bullying. Not for the first or last time, I feel that His Godship wants me to understand the word "irony" over and over again.

So I walk in and, for a second, I know what it feels to be Harry Potter. No, unfortunately I do not have the ability to cast down my enemies with a well-timed curse – but everyone is looking at me. Whispers hiss round the room. Even the teacher is a bit taken aback to see me. Did they all think that capital punishment was going to be my fate?

"Jess – welcome," Mr Morgan stutters. "Take a seat. We're looking at this photo and trying to work out the story behind it."

I say nothing and sit myself down next to Izzie. She mouths at me, "Okay?" Grateful for the first friendly word all day, I feel like crying. But instead I stare at the black and white photo in front of me. Behind me, Sana is hitting me in the back with a ruler, but I ignore her. I just don't want to talk. I just stare at the picture and ignore all the chatter around me.

And count the minutes to break.

I take refuge in our form room. The first topic of conversation is my interview with Mr Ambrose. There is outrage at my forced apology.

Suzie, all long hair and pout, says, "And you wrote it, Jess?"

I sigh. "I didn't want to. But it was that or being excluded. What would you have done? Anyway," I say, "I don't want to talk about that any more. I have better things to think about. For a start, me, Izzie and Hannah have been – wait for it – invited to Matt Paige's party."

Sighs, whispers of "How lucky are you!" ripple round the room.

At that moment, who comes waltzing in?

No, not the Ice Queen Zara, I don't think she's going to show her face just yet. No, it's her minions, Tara and Tiff. Tiff is in my form and Tara just stalks the school as if it's her territory. I secretly think she might wee in the corridor to mark her patch. She blasts the door open and then swivels to face us. She's on the verge of being over-emaciated like Cat, with huge eyes, cheekbones and pout. It's school, so her make-up is light but we can all spot Benefit a mile off – we might have a uniform but there are so many other ways to flaunt your wealth.

"What are you talking about?" she demands.

Suzie says, "Jess and crew have been invited to Matt Paige's party."

Tara is clearly not happy. Red spots flare on her cheeks and her eyes narrow. "And who invited you?" she says through compressed lips.

Hurrah – the first opportunity today to start enjoying myself. "Matt did."

She stares at me with her pretty but dead eyes. "Matt," she repeats.

"Yes, Matt," I say. "About six feet, pretty hot, friend of Hannah's brother – you know him?"

She bridles at this. "Of course I know him. I'm just a bit surprised he even knows who you are."

Izzie pipes up. "Well, everyone knows who Jess is now."

"What all the interest is, I've got no idea. All people should know about you is that you're famous for having fat legs. I'm not sure I'd want people to talk about that if I were you."

"Why?" I say. "Do you think your legs are fat?"

For a second, I wonder if she's going to slap me.

"Of course not," she mutters and turns to stalk out of the room. "You'll find that you won't know anyone at Matt's party. I think you'll find yourselves quite on your own. You might want to rethink going – you won't fit in." As she goes out, she sees little Bex in the corner, smirking at all this. "I don't know what you're laughing at. I'd look in a mirror and then see if I had anything to laugh about, if I were you. You're probably just about the ugliest girl in school. If you were a dog, you'd be put down."

Bex hangs her head and Zara smiles in triumph.

The door slams and we all rush over to Bex. "Ignore her, she's a cow," consoles Izzie.

Bex says quietly and without tears, "But she's right."

We don't know what to say. Thing is, all girls say they don't think they're pretty, and we all have bad days. Most girls at our school, either by good genes, good eating or good grooming, are actually okay to look at, though some are bigger and some smaller. But Bex doesn't fit with the pictures in the magazines at all. Her face is not regular. Her eyes are small, her teeth are crooked, her skin is bad. All these are things which could be fixed one way or another but she doesn't. In her way, she's more of a rebel than me.

I say, "She's *not* right. She's just a cow. You're worth twenty of her."

"But she's popular and I'm not," Bex says.

"How can she be popular when everyone hates her? She's part of this little group that think they're so great but no one else does."

"You've *got* to go to this party now," Suzie says. "You represent all us underdogs. You go and you snog some boy right in front of her!"

"Yeah," Sana laughs, her headscarf falling down around her ears, "I hear she's after Matt himself. Get him to snog you and then see her face." She LOLs at this and so does Suzie.

I feel uncomfortable for a moment and wonder if they're laughing because the idea of me snogging Matt is so ridiculous. Even Bex is laughing. For a moment, I see myself as they must see me. Funny, fat Jess. Always good for a giggle, always teasing the teacher, always eating. No one's idea of a pin-up. My head swirls again. I know I should eat something but the dress is always there in my mind.

I suddenly feel very tired. I'm fighting a war on so many fronts at the moment. At school with teachers and with bitches, at home with Mum and with the media, every time I open a magazine and see yet another photo that's guaranteed to make me feel rubbish about myself.

Worst of all, I seem to be at war with myself. And even I know that this just ain't gonna work. Something's gonna go tits over arse at some point – and it could well be me.

And if I think life will be simpler when I get home, think again. It's family meal night. God – you must be finding all of this really funny now.

Now our family meal night can be less than fun for a variety of reasons, as in most families. Family time is often thought to be good, because spending time together is a GOOD THING. It's not. Families should spend as little time together as possible.

So tonight's going to be even more weird than normal. I just hope that the ever-so-creepy Jack won't be there. That's the one thing I can do without.

By the time I get home, my head is spinning and my stomach hurts. It's only been one day without eating and I feel like I'm going mad. All I've had is an apple and Diet Coke all day and it's starting to show. Not where I want it to, round my tummy, bum and legs but in my temper, energy and eyes. But this is only Day One. I've got to give it a go.

I think about what to cook tonight. I'm beginning to realise why Cat is in such a foul mood pretty much all of the time. Because being hungry all the time absolutely sucks.

Normally I enjoy cooking, but tonight my heart's not in it. I bake white fish with ratatouille. There's some bread for those who want it. I add what flavour I can with garlic and fresh basil, plenty of salt. Salt may not be great for the heart but it's got hardly any calories and it tastes great. How many things can you say that about?

So about six thirty they all start to troop in.

The kitchen is full of rich, tomato smells. Hey, I've gone a bit wild and thrown some white wine in with the fish. Only a few calories and it's worth it for the flavour.

Dad says, "I've been looking forward to this all week. After today, we deserve a little treat? I know it's not Thai curry but it smells good." Dad loves Thai – I think he spent a long time there taking 'recreational' substances. He is his mother's son after all.

I serve it up. Five plates of fish in wine and lemon, and Mediterranean vegetables. No oil. No carbs. Just light protein and veggies.

Dad looks down at his plate and I think I'm about to see a grown man cry.

Lauren says, "That looks disgusting. Alice says it looks disgusting. She doesn't like vegetables and I don't like fish." She pushes the dish away with disgust. "When's pudding?"

I say nothing and begin to eat the bland meal.

Dad says quietly, "Is there any sauce?"

I shake my head. He nods and begins to eat slowly and without any enthusiasm.

Mum and Cat eat quietly without comment. I think that I just miss a flash of eye contact between them. I refuse to look at them.

If I was on *Master Chef*, what would Nick and the fat one say? "The vegetables are soft, pleasant in texture and full of flavour. The fish is well seasoned and light. However, the whole thing lacks substance and creativity. It is not the worst meal that I have ever eaten in my life. But it's far from the best."

But it is food. And I'm hungry, so it is gone far too quickly and I still want more at the end.

I finish first. Lauren and Alice are arguing about which exactly is the most disgusting vegetable on their plate. Dad looks sad. Mum and Cat are eating in exactly the same way that drives me mad – small bite, chew twenty times, swallow, drink water, repeat.

Mum starts, "This is very pleasant . . ."

"Thanks," I reply.

"It's a bit different from what you normally cook," she says. "What's the inspiration behind it?" I look to see if she's laughing at me cos if she is I will take a kebab skewer and plant it right between her eyes.

"Summer," I lie. "The weather's getting warmer and I thought a light meal would be nice."

To her credit, Mum just nods and says nothing.

Cat doesn't have such tact. "Are you trying to lose weight?" she says.

Part of me is reeling because Cat has actually said something. Part of me is reeling cos Cat has hit on the truth and I don't want to admit it. I know it's extreme, but I think I would rather die than admit the truth to her.

"Are you saying I'm fat?" I reply.

She shrugs. "I'm just asking."

"Do you like it?" I ask. "That should be the only reason to eat food."

She tuts at this and stops eating.

"Are you full?" I say.

"I've had enough," she replies.

"That's not what I asked," I push.

She stands up and walks out of the room.

Mum glances at me. She pauses. "Jess. Firstly, I'd like to thank you for cooking such a lovely meal. But you could be more sensitive. You know it's a difficult subject for her."

I feel like crying. It's just food – where did it get so complicated?

There is silence.

Then Dad asks, "What's for pudding?"

I look him in the eye. "Fresh fruit and fresh air." I listen hard; I think I hear his heart break. And probably mine too.

Chapter 15

Invisible Rule № 11: People can get a bit funny if you use the F-word. No, not that F-word. I mean "feminist". But you can be a feminist without having hairy pits, wearing sensible shoes and snogging every girl who comes your way.

After dinner, I go to my room to do some homework. I mean, if I'm actually going to be allowed to sit my GCSEs then I suppose I should do some work. At least it keeps me occupied.

My phone pings. I look at the screen. It's MATT.

Hey, got into any fights today?

Heart pounding, I reply.

Nope, not yet. But will start practising mud wrestling later. ☺

LOL – sounds fun. Send me a photo if you do. ;-)

But then I'm distracted as Lauren comes in, all sobbing, and gets into my bed.

I wonder what Alice has done to her now.

"What's up, shrimp?" I ask her. "This is not a good time."

I quickly type out, *Sure. Am in my Lycra suit already.*

"I don't want to get married," Lauren sobs into my pillow. She's four. WTF?

"Why are you thinking about marriage?" I ask her. My phone is dead. He's not responding. What did I say?

"It's the end of *The Little Mermaid*." She shudders and sits up. "Ariel gets married and goes off and leaves her daddy behind. I don't want to leave home, I don't want to leave you, I want to stay here forever."

With that, she hiccups and cries big snotty tears. I hug her and try to avoid the snot. How messed up can you get? I mean, Disney cartoons can be so wrong on so many levels, but I'd think a huge half-woman/half-octopus is scarier than marriage (note the message – fat woman is evil . . .). I stroke her hair. "Lauren, you can stay here forever. No one has to get married unless they want to. You don't have to get married."

I keep looking at my phone but the display remains dark. I stroke Lauren's hair as I think over those texts again and again. Maybe he's just busy. And he was the first to text, after all.

Lauren seems to calm down a bit at this. And then falls asleep in my bed. I look at her in wonder. I wish I could fall asleep like that. And I wish I could be four. No rampaging hormones that make you behave like a cave woman when you're really aiming for a more sophisticated look. Four years olds don't worry about what they look like or if boys like them. Or spend half an hour pondering every possible meaning that a text message could have.

I'm hungry. I think about where I can go where there's no food. Granny. She never eats. So I carry Lauren, snoring, back to her bed and I go up and see Granny. She's watching *The Maltese Falcon*. I like this one. Sam Spade is cool and the women are awesome, all attitude. I do like films like this. If I had a waist I'd put on some super slim jacket, paint my nails and lips red, start to smoke and get myself into some ungodly mess.

"Ah, Jesobel, my love," she murmurs when she sees me. I lean over and kiss her papery soft cheek. "Get your old granny a top up and get one for yourself. Only a half, mind," and she winks.

"Top half or bottom half?" I ask with a smile. This is Granny's favourite joke when pouring a drink.

"Always the top!" she says. I pour her a generous portion of whisky and pop in three ice cubes from the freezer compartment of her little fridge. She nods approvingly.

I have my own special glass. It's a long shot glass with various levels painted on it in old fashioned gilt writing, now badly faded. I still know what it says, even though you can't read it. It's a joke. The lowest measure is Ladies, next comes Gentlemen (sexist), and then two pictures, Little Pig and Big Pig. I pour vodka up to Ladies and then start to add the Coke. I mean, I know it's full of calories, but vodka and Diet Coke isn't too many and I've hardly eaten anything all day.

I just have one – it's a thing I do with Gran. Makes me feel grown up.

Gran stares closely at me. "Next one should be a Big Pig," she says. "You look like you need it."

I look at her profile. She doesn't seem that much like Dad. I've seen pictures of Granddad. He died before I was born and he doesn't look much like Dad either.

I sit at Gran's feet and lean against her. She strokes my hair. I feel like crying.

I tell her about Lauren and the Little Mermaid.

Gran snorts. "You should tell her the real story, the one where he marries someone else and it's torture, every step she takes. Now *that's* a story to cry about. Too highly strung, that child. Full of nonsense." She takes a sip. "But then maybe she instinctively knows that marriage is a way to repress women. She might have a point after all."

"She's only four," I remind her.

"When I was four, I got a hard smack on the bottom for silliness and frankly that child is silly at times. She lives in a fantasy world – she needs to face reality!" Gran knocks back the contents of her glass and asks for more.

"What's it like being married?" I ask to distract her.

She looks at me with a steely glare. "Why, are you thinking of giving it a go?" she says. "Patriarchal nonsense. Why should a woman change her name and just become a piece of property to a man?" She pauses, still searching my face. "But why are you asking? You're not thinking of getting married, are you, Jesobel? If you are, I'll come and put a stop to it PDQ."

This makes me smile. I know she must sometimes, cos she has to go to the loo, but she's not been seen out of this room in three years.

"No," I say. "I've just been thinking."

"Both thinking and feeling are overrated in my book," Gran says crisply. "Best to just get on and make the most of things."

"Is that comment related to marriage?" I continue.

Gran pauses. "Perhaps." She sighs. "I loved your granddad, but he was hard work. Marriage is tiresome. It just wears you out after a while. We only got married because I got pregnant anyway, and it made our tax situation easier. So even I've conformed from time to time."

She turns to Humphrey Bogart. He's quizzing the bad guy. Life looks more glamorous and less complicated in black and white.

"The whisky helps," she says.

"You do know I'm too young to drink, and that you drink too much?" I say. Which is true. I'm buzzing from the vodka, especially with only fish and vegetables inside me. Has Gran been topping my drink up when I've not been looking?

"Pish, I was at parties every week when I was your age. Started going to protests then, too. Got a bit tipsy from time to time. It wasn't the drink that was bad for me, it was the marriage."

Her eyes go bright for a moment. "I don't know what they mean by *drinking too much*. I'm an old lady with few pleasures. And two of them are in the room at the moment." She strokes my hair again.

"There's so much I don't know about your life, Gran," I say.

"You can't even guess," she smiles. "But I'll tell you one secret if you like."

"Go on," I say. She nods towards her bureau, which has drawers and things where she puts stuff. "Third drawer down," she says, holding out a small key with her ancient hands.

I carefully take the key from her, unlock the drawer and pull it open. I take out an old photo, all curled and yellow round the edges. A cool looking brunette with clever eyes smiles out from it. She's wearing denim and her arm is around a younger version of Gran.

"That's the only person I ever really loved," she says.

I think I spit out my drink.

"But . . ." I splutter. "But . . ."

"Yes, I know she's a woman. But that's where my heart led me. For a time."

She smiles at my open mouth.

"So your silly old Gran isn't quite what you thought. You

have no idea, really, my darling, about what my life's been like. One day we need to have a proper talk. Now, enough of this talking, pour me another drink and get yourself one while you're at it."

So we play cards and drink. I've eaten pretty much nothing all day so no surprise that the room starts reeling after a while. My grandmother? A lesbian? Or bi? I don't even know what the label is. I know it shouldn't matter but I can't quite take it all in. I mean, I don't have a problem with girls who like girls – I'm just never quite sure how to react. Though I do remember being in Year Seven when two Year Eleven girls were snogging in the dining room and Mrs Brown nearly had a coronary.

Eventually, I head off to my bedroom. Just as I get into bed, my phone buzzes. I wonder who that could be at this time of night. The precious letters *MATT* shine at me in the darkness. He's texted me. Again.

Am I imagining this?

With mind and heart pounding, I drunkenly start to stab at the buttons.

Chapter 16

Invisible Rule № 12: All fun stuff – food, alcohol, etc. – is bad for you. It's God's idea of a joke. The exception is sex – sex with a condom, of course. But there must be less complicated ways of burning calories. I mean, you're never going to lose sleep over whether a cross-trainer likes you or not.

In the morning, it's official – I feel like pure human excrement.

I remember talking to Granny. I remember drinking vodka with her. I poured myself one. One! But how come I feel like this . . .? I do remember Gran grabbing the bottle from time to time. Maybe she thought it would make me feel better to have a few drinks. She wasn't to know I'd hardly eaten all day. We played cards. And then it all goes a bit blurry TBH. There's like a black hole in my head (along with the aching void in my stomach).

But what's eating away at me (oh the irony!) is the feeling that I've forgotten something. I get the sense that I did something or something happened between me lurching down the stairs from Granny's and then collapsing on my bed. Cos, have I forgotten to mention it? I'm still wearing the clothes I was wearing last night. Classy! Yep, I've gone for the full mascara down the face, sweaty, crumpled look. At least I've not weed in my bed or anything like that, like Amy Dutton did after Michael Wood's party last year.

My phone is lying on the floor next to the bed. I look at it. OMG.

OMFG.

OMFFFG.

I think I'm going to be sick. What unholy combination of lack of food and excessive vodka led to thist? I had a whole text conversation with Matt last night. And what a conversation. It's not just that I'm full on flirting with him. It's not just that he's full on flirting with me. It's not just that he's telling me to send him "something interesting".

No, it's that I used my camera phone. And sent him a photo. And it's not the kind your parents put on the mantelpiece to show Great Aunt Sally when she comes round. I know other girls who've sent sexts. But not me.

I don't feel much like talking for a while. I need the bathroom.

Next thing I know I'm being sick. At least I make it to the loo this time.

BRB.

There's not much funny stuff to put about sitting on the bathroom floor retching your guts up on your own, especially when you've just realised you've drunkenly sent a picture of your boobs to a guy you hardly know. I mean, it would be funny if it were someone else, right? But I'm experiencing a strange lack of humour at the present. I think I could turn this into an equation. The less food that goes into my body, this less funny the whole world becomes.

After a shower, endless teeth brushing and as much Paracetamol as I can take, I look myself firmly in the eye. I can just say I've got a bug. I look like I've got a bug. I look like I've eaten several bugs and now they're eating me from the inside. Who's he sent that picture to? By the time I get to school, will the entire world have seen the picture?

I stumble down the stairs. The kitchen is blissfully quiet. Lauren is watching CBeebies, eating Frosties; Mum's in the shower; Dad won't be up much before ten. No one ever knows where Cat is.

I sigh. On one level, I want to drink my black coffee in peace, without anyone quizzing me over what I'm having for breakfast. But on the other hand, I want Dad to come in and look sad and question me over my eating habits. I want someone in my family to notice that something's changed. But no – in this house, we all stumble on dysfunctionally and just wallow around in our own mess and no one seems to put out a hand to help each other.

I feel hot tears run down my face. I don't know whether

to tell Hannah and Izzie what I've done. What has Matt done with the photo? Stomach lurching, I check on the web. Nothing on my page. Nothing on Matt's page. So, nothing yet. Yet. But it's out there and there's nothing I can do to get it back. Maybe I should text him, but I don't have the words.

At a sound behind me, I wipe away my tears. Mum bustles in. "Coffee – fab," she breezes.

She peers at me. "You look a bit peaky," she says.

"Just feel a bit rubbish today," I say, looking sad.

She looks concerned. "You could take the day off, but after yesterday's meeting . . . I suppose you should go in if you can."

I think about a day spent in bed. It seems the most appealing thing in the world. But then I'd be on my own and currently I just don't really like my own company so much. So I smile. "No, Mum, it's fine, I'll go in. I'll ring at lunchtime if I'm still feeling rubbish."

She hugs me. "Fine. I'll check on you later." Then she rushes out, coffee in her hand. "Lauren, why are you still in your pyjamas? It's time for nursery!"

There is wailing. Normally I'd smile but this morning I can't.

At the corner of the street, Hannah is waiting for me. She's full of giggles and jumping around. I am not. "What's up, babes?" she asks. Clearly I look as sad as I feel.

I shrug off all enquiries. So we walk to school, with her doing all the talking and me wondering how I can raise the money to run off and live in Australia. The airport's only thirty minutes away by bus. I could be over another continent by lunchtime if it all goes tits up. But that's hardly the right expression under the circumstances . . .

Normally, as we walk to school and slowly start to mingle with pupils from the boys' school, it's a good morning if I get some attention from the boys. But this time, I'm watching all their faces for one flicker that suggests they're laughing at me behind my back. One snigger and I'm on the bus, and Bondi Beach, here I come. But no. Sure, Fred and Dom come over for a chat, but all they want to talk about is whether I've seen Zara.

"Shame," says Fred when I tell them that I haven't. "I was looking forward to more scandal." Then he tells me about how a boy lost it in the form room and started throwing chairs about. I can't imagine that happening at our school.

"But no one got to film it in time. Shame – it was really funny."

But as he says it, I think that it probably wasn't funny for the boy. He must have been furious about something. Why should that be shared with the rest of the world? I mean, my clip seemed funny at the time but now the joke has worn well and truly thin. Thin . . . that word just keeps getting every-where. If I'd eaten properly yesterday, I wouldn't be in this mess. And then there's the vodka. I think that might have had something to do with it.

By the time we get to school, I feel slightly better. Matt hasn't done anything with the photo. Yet.

Maybe he won't.

He's a decent guy.

He does Art A-level.

And he writes poetry.

He won't do the dirty on me.

I hope.

Chapter 17

Invisible Rule № 13: Never tell the truth. I mean, really, don't.
No one ever really wants to hear it. Just tell yourself the truth.

So first lesson of the day is PE. You might think that as a larger person I might hate PE, but I do like to confound and confuse if I can.

See, normally PE can be fun. Stay with me. Cos it's fun to see how serious some people can be about an activity that is essentially moving a ball around. Yep, let's think about that for a moment – sport is usually about moving a vaguely spherical object from one location to the next while making it as complicated as possible. This is true for football, rugby, netball, cricket and golf, to name but a few. It's similar with athletics. How can we move from one place to the next as quickly as possible, often placing irrelevant obstacles in the way to make it harder? Some call this challenging yourself. I call it stupid.

So I find PE amusing for these reasons and also because this is when all the various elements of the school come together in a context that involves direct rather than indirect competition. The sporty, the fashion conscious, the swots and the geeks – all present, and all worlds collide. Often literally.

But I'm not finding much amusing today. In my head, I keep thinking over those texts from last night. I honestly don't remember a thing and yet the evidence is there in my phone. Hopefully not for all to see. Some shot of my boobs, taken by me, (unless some random phone pixie managed to do it to me while I was asleep) is now out there. In cyberspace. And there's not a thing I can do about it. I mean, it's one thing having the most boring IT teacher give some assembly on keeping yourself cybersafe. Oh yes, I sat there in Year Eight with everyone else, thinking, *What a loser! Only an idiot would take a dodgy picture of themselves and send it out there.* Well, who's the loser and the idiot now?

And how does this leave me feeling about Matt? It's not exactly romantic, is it, to ask for that kind of shot? Not sure how all of this adds up to him being perfect boyfriend material. I think of the most romantic movie I know – *Romeo and Juliet* (I know it's a play too but frankly the play sucks in comparison). Romeo, especially played by Leonardo diCaprio when he was actually pretty, wouldn't do this. (Partly cos phones weren't invented then, I suppose.)

"Come on, ladies, let's get lively!" Our PE teacher bounces up and down like a hyperactive terrier. "Jess, at least I won't have to send you to the Head today for uniform infringement." She looks at my regulation PE skirt and laughs. I don't crack a smile. Though part of my brain – the bit that's still capable of thought – does process this. Two days ago my short skirt = rebellion and chaos. Now my short skirt = uniform. Context is everything.

While she witters on about rules and technique, I think about calories. I was going to have a run this morning but what with the hangover and phone revelation to cope with, that went out the window. So this is a good opportunity to burn some fat.

And then we're off. Thirty girls, some of whom really don't like each other, are armed with lethal pieces of wood and let loose on each other. There's a TV series to be made here. Put us in a skimpy outfit and we'd be TV gold. It's like mortal combat out there some days. It would be truly scary if we were all as ramped up as Sporty Amy who plays as if every kitten in the world will be impaled upon spikes unless she gives it her all. But she's not alone today. As the part of my brain that has gone into calorie-counting mode realises how many calories I could burn up, I suddenly find myself running around like a crazy person too. Which I am.

Forty minutes later, I am feeling wobbly. My stomach hurts, my brain's numb and my hands are shaking. This is only Day Two. How will I ever make the next two weeks and one day? I tell myself that these feelings are good. That it's working. That to be hungry is good.

"Are you okay?" Hannah says, as I prop myself up on the hockey stick.

"Yes. Just might be going down with a bug," I say.

I don't think that she quite believes me but she's too good a friend to disagree. I stagger off the field and get changed.

The rest of the day is a blur. Then form room at lunchtime. Normally I would be tucking in to my home-prepared lunch. No mass produced crap pretending to be healthy crap from the dining hall for me. Only now I'm not eating anything.

Hannah looks closely at me. "Where's your lunch?"

I have put some thought into how to answer this question. I need to be vaguely plausible. "With all the stress this morning, I forgot. I'll pick up something later."

Izzie looks so shocked that she actually stops reapplying her mascara for a second.

I give her the stare. "I refuse to eat anything that this school makes. It's a matter of principle. Anyway," I shrug, "I'm hardly going to waste away."

Then an animated expression takes hold of her. She stares at me. "You do look odd, you know. And you've not really been eating much. OMG. She's doing some weird spell on you."

"What are you talking about?" I say.

"Zara, of course. She hates you, we all know that. Maybe she's hired someone to put a curse on you. I mean, you not eating is just not normal. You have to admit that."

I'm about to say, *No, I am eating – just not very much*, but then this would be admitting that I'm on a diet. Me. Who has mocked every single girl in this school who has ever said this. Every girl who has mentioned the word "calories". Every girl who has been sad about food or their weight.

How can I explain that I have gone on a diet just to try and impress a boy?

I can explain this, or I can let Izzie continue with this madness that I am affected by an evil spirit. TBH, it's all a bit much.

And that's when I black out.

Chapter 18

(Sort of. This is less of a chapter than a montage. Don't sue –
just chill!)

Invisible Rule № 14: This is an ironic rule – there isn't one. See what I did there ;-)

1. If this was a film, this would be the bit where there would be a montage of lots of pictures of me looking sad, not eating, hugging cushions, checking my phone like a crazy woman and staring into the middle distance while some woman yodels over a slow piano arrangement. In the cinema, you'd either be wiping a tear from your eye or thinking this is boring so you might as well go for a wee.
2. But it's not a film. So here goes.
3. I fainted. Too much PE, too much stress, too little food. You don't need to be a genius to work out what was going on there.
4. I come round, they take me to the nurse, she asks me lots of questions, I tell lots of lies. Dad comes to pick me up. He looks worried, but not worried enough to stop winking at the nurse and signing an autograph for her. Turns out she's a fan of his one-hit wonder.
5. We go home. I don't eat dinner.
6. I go to bed but I can't sleep cos I'm hungry, so I eat a small salad and some fruit.
7. I get up for school the next day. I don't eat much.
8. My head hurts, my stomach hurts, I feel like I want to die but I keep on not eating. I'm not sure why.
9. The dress hangs in the corner of my room. It smiles at me.
10. I think I am losing weight but I can't bear to weigh

myself. I know from past experience that the scales never give you the answer you want. It's either too much. Or if you *have* lost something, it's never enough.

11. But my clothes are starting to feel looser.

12. School is a blur. With our exams coming up fast, the teachers just test us to destruction. Mock, timed essay, assessment. The little energy I have goes into keeping my hand continually moving.

13. Instead of eating, I revise. And revise and revise and then revise a bit more.

14. Every day of not eating is torture. But every day takes me closer to the party. In my head I have imagined every possibility. I like the ones where Matt swears his love for me in front of everyone there, while Zara stands, ignored by all, in the corner.

15. I don't see or hear from Matt, and have no idea how he feels about me. The photo doesn't appear anywhere. Which is good. I feel I should like him less for asking for it. But I don't. Every waking hour, and most of my dreams, I'm thinking about him. #stalker

16. The days go by. And then – then, finally – it's time for the party.

And it's like my life can start again.

Chapter 19

*Invisible Rule № 15: If a boy sleeps with a girl, he's cool. If a girl
sleeps with a boy, she's a slut.*

Today is the day. The day of the party. The day that my life
seems to have been focused on forever.

I don't know how much weight I've lost but I figure that
today I can eat. Finally.

I open our fridge. Dad pretends to be environmentally
friendly but that didn't stop him and Mum buying the biggest badass fridge known to humankind. Even Americans
might find our fridge excessive. I keep opening it and expecting some penguins, Caribou and the last Inuit tribe to come
wandering out. Fortunately, all I find are the ingredients for
scrambled egg, smoked salmon and bagels.

I put on some coffee, blast out some Beyoncé, split the bagels, crack out the butter, slightly salted, and begin to make
the best scrambled eggs this side of the Pennines. A dash of
cream, a shaving of cheese, these babies are gonna be fab!

I pile it all high, first the bagel, with a slab of butter, then
the salmon, as much as I can bear, then the hot, salty, slightly
cheesy eggs. I breathe in deeply for a moment and then begin
to eat.

The heat, flavour and salt explode in my mouth. The butter
starts to melt and the glorious burst of salt and fat makes my
body sing. For a few minutes, my mouth is in ecstasy and my
stomach slowly begins to sing hallelujahs as it begins to realise that normal service has been resumed. I'm not sure that I
feel happy, but I am starting to feel full.

Dad comes in and looks at my plate. "Looks good, kid," he
says.

"It is," I say, "I made it."

"Any left for your old dad?"

"I can make some more," I say. "But you'll have to wait."

He goes to the iPod and searches through. He finds Oasis, Blur, all guys who were doing the business when he was. His finger stops scanning. He finds his song. He looks at me; I smile.

"I like it, Dad – it's one of my faves. So put it on and turn it up."

So Dad blasts it out and smiles at me while I make him the best brunch I can manage.

"You're a better guitarist than Noel Gallagher," I say.

He smiles. "God hates a liar."

My phone goes. I let Hannah and Izzie know that I am conscious and ready to party. This is not true. Parties are generally considered fun events, and yet my stomach is currently deciding whether to enjoy the hearty and delicious breakfast that I have lovingly made or reject it and see it slide all over the granite worktops.

I did have strange dreams about Matt all night (Well most nights TBH). One was particularly bizarre, where we were about to be shipwrecked and then a large shark ate him. I could look on an online dream website to find out what that was all about, or I could just trust my instinct. The shark did have a look of Zara about it. All teeth and dead eyes.

I go upstairs. I need a plan. Do I shower now?? And then again?? This is not the night to be in any doubt about my level of cleanliness. You don't want to be having an intimate moment and then it all go horribly wrong cos the guy's gagging over your sweat problem.

Izzie's arrived, complete with candles, incense and hair straighteners. Bless her little heart. We're getting ready here rather than the cellar cos there's more room and easier access to a bathroom. As this process could take hours, we need space and comfort!

She sits on my bed and looks uncharacteristically nervous.

"When is Hannah getting here?" she says.

"Soon," I reply. "What's up?"

She makes a face as if deciding to tell me something. "So . . . what if I liked Alex?" she says.

For a moment, I have no idea who she means. She tries

again, patiently. "As in, ginger Alex, Hannah's brother?"

I think about this. He's a perfectly decent guy. Not that hot, but then not hideous. I've never really thought of him like that. I've known him all my life, so he's always just been there.

"Why not? Does he know you like him?"

"I don't know. We talk quite a lot. He keeps hinting that he really likes someone. I'm just not sure if it's me or not." She pauses. "The thing is I just think he might think I'm a bit – you know – common. That I'm chavvy."

I look at her in amazement. "Why would he ever think that?" I say.

"I don't speak like you, I don't live in a big house, I've never been to the theatre. The only theatre I'd ever heard of before I came to St Etheldreda's was Old Trafford – the Theatre of Dreams. You have no idea how hard it is – I love you guys but do you never wonder why I never invite you round?"

The worst bit about this is that I have never really thought about Izzie's home life.

She continues, "The stupid thing is that where I live they think I'm a snob. But at school, I sound so common. And on parents' evening, all the mums look at my mum like she's a chav. I really, really like Alex. I don't think he looks down on me. Do you think that I have a chance with him?"

I'm about to say that I think that she's got better odds of snogging Alex than I do Matt but at this moment Hannah arrives with more make-up than I've ever seen in my life. Izzie silences me with a look and the moment is over.

We look at the mound of stuff on my bed.

Checklist:

1. Magazines, telling us all we need to know about looking like a hot girl.
2. All the make-up that we either own or have secretly borrowed from our mums.
3. Clothes that will transform us from ordinary girls into goddesses that boys will want to snog and then our lives will be complete. Hmmm.

Izzie says, "I'd like to do a ceremony before we start."

Hannah and I look at each other.

"Now before you two roll your eyes, I want you to remember that we are all friends and, as such, we should respect each other's ideas. If you don't like what I'm about to propose, then just think of it as either positive energy or, worst case scenario, an opportunity to laugh at me. All I'll say is – remember Rebecca Turner."

We do. We remember that Izzie thinks that she arranged that unlikely union. A union as unlikely as me and Matt Paige.

"I'm in," I say.

"Me too," Hannah follows. "What do we do?"

Izzie should be a theatre director! She shuts the curtains, she lights a ring of red candles and Hannah and I sit at two points of a triangle. Izzie makes the final point and throws red petals in the middle as she hums some weird tune.

"Take a candle," she then commands.

We do.

"Repeat after me," she says.

We do.

"Spirits wild and spirits free
Look on us, a willing three.
In our hearts lies secret love
Grant our wishes from above."

I'm not sure if the spirits are poetry critics, but if they are then I think they might find this a bit rubbish.

"In your third eye, see the face of the one you love. Visualise it as intensely as you can."

I think of Matt looking up at me that first night I saw him, how his long hair fell into his dark eyes, the smile that played round the corners of his lips and his eyes. How, for a second, I felt a complete connection with him and how I've replayed this moment over and over again. I hold on to this, as if wishing will somehow bring him into the room.

On the count of three, we blow out our candles. We sit in the gloom for a minute. We wait. Izzie gets up and opens the curtains. "That should do it," she says.

I remind them, "We've got a party to go to and we've got to look great."

It begins.

I'm sent for a shower, while Izzie and Hannah scour the mags for ideas. Then comes the tricky business of getting rid of pretty much all your body hair. Cos whilst the hair on your head is supposedly to be long and glossy, God help you if there's any other hair ANYWHERE else! Any dark hairs on limbs or under limbs or unmentionable places *must* be removed. Option a) close encounter with a razor (danger – stubble alert!) or option b) wax. Waxing is made to look so easy in adverts but last time I tried, I stuck myself to the duvet.

So in these circumstances, a girl's best friend is Veet. It's pink, it smells funny and it dissolves your hair. Not particularly natural, but then neither are hair-free legs. I'm wearing skinny jeans so I'm not quite sure why I think my legs should be hair free but you don't suddenly want to find yourself in a position where hair-free legs might be a good idea and then shout out, "Hang on a minute, keep that thought, I'm just going to the bathroom and excuse the industrial smell when I get back."

So I'm doing it now. Just In Case.

So I smear thick pink gloop over my legs up to and including my bikini line. Then I smear all over my armpits. Not much going on there, but I may as well do a proper job. Now I have to wait five minutes. Only I've forgotten to put the timer on and now I've got to set the timer with slippy pink fingers. I wonder if the gloop will dissolve my phone so I wipe the stuff off my fingers on to the towel (Mum will love me) and then try to wipe it off my phone without cancelling the timer. This is not a good start.

I'm sat naked in my bathroom, perched on the edge of the loo, covered in pink gloop, waiting for the phone ring.

I hope this is not a symbol of my life to come.

There is little dignity in this moment but it's the end result that I'm hoping for.

I play a few songs on my phone and check out the buzz on the party tonight.

I jump when the harp rings out to tell me that it's time. I take my little scrapey bit of plastic and scrape as if my life depends on it. A few rebellious hairs refuse to go. I'll get them on Phase Two with the razor.

I shower at length. My skins feels great, thanks to the super-strength conditioner they put into the gloop. No hair on legs or under arms. I clearly went a bit mad on the bikini line as now I seem to have given myself a homemade Hollywood. I've turned myself into a porn star! I can hardly stick it back on so I'm left with a small triangle of hair.

Okay, all bad hair gone. Now the good hair! This gets washed three times, followed by two conditioning treatments.

I think I'm done. I put on my PJs and dressing gown . Hair first, then make-up.

Izzie does a great job with my hair. My once wavy locks are poker straight and shiny. In another twenty minutes, Hannah's hair is a set of stunning red curls. Izzie even manages to transform her fake black hair into glossy dark curls that any Hollywood star would be proud of.

Then it's time for smoky smokin' hot eyes, lip gloss and the works. We look in the mirror together. Result – three girls who look like girls in a magazine. Hannah and Izzie giggle. I gasp.

It doesn't look like me in the mirror. My eyes are normally a bit small and podgy. Now they look huge, and they blaze brightly. My whole face looks different. Big eyes, big lips, big hair.

I peer closely and me and then back away. The reflection does exactly what I do. This girl in the mirror clearly is me, but it's a better version of me. An airbrushed, perfect, plastic me.

I wish I could look like this all the time. .

Hannah, Izzie and I look at each other and we smile. We all look great, no one needs to boost anyone's ego, no one looks better than the others. We are all as hot as we'll ever be.

Our makeover has delivered its first goal. We are a step further away from being ourselves. But does that bring us anywhere nearer to what we want?

The final part – getting dressed. As this point, I feel sick to my stomach. Yes, I look pretty. But then no one has ever really said that I'm ugly. So that's not the issue. The issue has always been . . . fat.

I stare at the wardrobe. I can almost hear the dress laughing at me, teasing me for dreaming that I could wear it and not look ridiculous. I've not dared try it on yet and I don't want to put it on in front of them. If all my fat is still hanging out, it's too much to bear, even in front of my best friends.

As if Hannah senses my anxiety, she says, "I just want to call Suzie about a few things. I'll be back in a minute." Then Izzie decides to go to the toilet. So it's just me and the dress.

Who cares about winning some kind of competition with an inanimate object? Apparently I do. Mum has thoughtfully bought me a pair of Spanx. I believe Adele swears by them. So that's okay. Why go on a diet when you can just damage your internal organs by encasing them in gut-busting elastic?

I open the wardrobe. The dress glows in the dark, its pink softness alluring. It's not quite what I'd normally wear and the danger is that it's not quite the same as what everyone else will wear, but over black skinny jeans, it looks like something out of Vogue. I don't have a backup, there's no Plan B. If it doesn't fit, I don't know what I'll do.

I take a deep breath. I put on my jeans and zip them up. Then I pull the dress over my head. It slips down. For a moment I can't bear to look at myself in the mirror.

And then I do.

I feel like crying.

It fits. It looks good.

I'm not thin but I'm thinner. I almost look normal. I look more like Mum; I could look like Cat. I might not be top of anyone's snog list but I wouldn't be an embarrassment. I stare at myself in disbelief. Is this what they mean when they say that nothing tastes as good as skinny feels? I've always dismissed this as nonsense in the past, but now I begin to get what they mean.

There's a knock at the door. I let Izzie in.

She gasps, "You've lost so much weight! Oh, Jess, you look lovely – but are you okay?"

Hannah comes through the door, looking flushed. She stops for a moment. "Wow," is all she says.

It's enough.

"Are we just about ready?" I say.

We nod, but it's too early. No one will get there until later and we don't want to look too keen. Time for dancing! We turn up the speakers and start to practise our moves to Rihanna.

We don't notice the knock at the door. We don't notice anything until the flash dazzles us. We turn and see Mum in the doorway, phone in hand.

"You all look beautiful," she says quietly.

She looks at me with a kind of intensity that's embarrassing. But it's nice. For once.

But enough of the soppy stuff – who wants a moment with your mum when you could be out with your friends, getting drunk and snogging a fit boy?

"Come on!" I yell.

We get to the cellar. Too many parents in my house. We dance and drink and text and Facebook and tweet.

There's a rap at the door and there's Dom and Fred. They bunch together on the recliner and our pre-party goes from strength to strength. Firstly, they're boys; secondly, they like us; and thirdly, it's always better to go to a party as part of a crowd. Makes you look like you've got the whole world as your friends.

By now we are buzzing and the boys are staring at us greedily. Any other night and I might be tempted. Either would do. But tonight I don't want to settle for okay. Tonight I want the strange, complicated fantasy in my head to become reality.

It's time to go. Outside the lights begin to blur and dance as we spin down the street. Suddenly, jumping over dog poo is funny. Spinning round lampposts even funnier. I am feel that Dom is close to me – never going far, breathing down my neck. All of a sudden the night has all kinds of possibilities.

Fred is tailing Hannah in the same way and Izzie is just dancing along, clearly amused by all of this.

We twist and turn along the familiar streets of our childhood. Beyond the large terraced houses the summer sky glows with the last burn of golden light and the pale blue sky arches over us. I think of the song Dad plays for us at summer barbecues, from the time when I was born and he was still playing gigs. It always makes me think of evenings like this, of perfect summer skies and endless possibilities. That's how I want my life to be.

We all get the giggles as we suddenly realise that we're not sure of the number of Matt's house, but before we get round to texting anyone, we just listen out for the noise, and then we hear the bass and then we see the people ringing the door bell, and we know that we've found the right place.

Chapter 20

Jess Observation № 5: Rules are there to be broken.

We ring the doorbell and it's opened by Cat, of all people. She never said she was coming! But that's Cat for you. She looks me up and down and nods with vague approval. I feel like getting someone to take a photograph of the two of us – to capture a rare moment where Cat doesn't treat me with contempt.

"I'll let you in," she says and then we burst through and get our first glimpse of Matt's house. It's huge – much bigger than ours – and I can't believe his parents have let him have a party. It's like being in a magazine like *Cheshire Life*. Each piece of furniture looks like it's just come from an antique shop; but then it looks too perfect, not like a home.

We girls head for the music and the front room while the boys are sent on a mission to find us a drink.

The room is pulsing with sound. My ears hurt, but my feet want to dance. There's a small group of bodies, weaving and stomping in the centre of the room. Around the edge, in huge chairs and sofas, more bodies are strewn. Some are girls, entangled with each other, looking out at the action. Others are couples, all roving hands and winding tongues, eyes shut. I try to see if any are Matt, without looking like some perv who likes watching other people snog.

I can't see him anywhere. But the music is calling me and so Dom grabs my hand and we start to dance. For a while, it feels like the best thing – the music pounding through me, friendly faces, Dom staring at me longingly. I'm happy when I dance, don't care if I'm good or bad. I'm not out to impress anyone, I just want to move and feel the groove and, for a while, that's enough.

Then someone changes the music and it gets grungy. I

don't hate it, but I can't dance to it. Someone shoves a glass of something in my hand. I begin to feel a bit on edge. The glow is going off the day. Izzie is deep in debate with some guy about whether magic is real or not. He's clearly teasing her but she's giving as good as she gets and they're both having a good time. Can't see Hannah, so I decide to go and try and find her – it gives me something to do and also gives me a chance to find Matt.

As I wander through the large hallway, I catch a glimpse of a tall blonde girl with smoky eyes, a pink dress and black jeggings. It takes a second for it to sink in that it's me, my reflection, caught in a long mirror.

I pull myself together and avoid the snogging couple sitting on the telephone table, as the telephone sadly beeps to itself on the floor. They seem to be having sex with their clothes on – at least it's safe, but it looks like they're gonna get clothes burns. "Get a room," I say as I pass.

I drift into the kitchen. Cat is standing with a gaggle of tall boys around her, who are taking it in turns to make her laugh. But where's Jack? Is that why she's happy, cos he's not here? It's nice, though weird, to see her laughing. I decide to give her a wide berth but I do want a drink, so I sneak in. The kitchen's huge, so I can get to the fridge without going too near them.

"That's my sister," I hear Cat call and I turn, unsure of what reception I'm going to get. She is smiling as she looks at me and I can detect no obvious signs of menace. The boys all are smiling too, and again I don't smell a trap. "So have you been creating any more crazy clips lately?" one says, and as this seems my cue to go and talk to them, so I do.

I quite like the next twenty minutes or so. It's like I'm in some kind of spotlight that makes life sparkly. They laugh when I retell my story. Cat listens and laughs in the right places. She doesn't make me look like a fool, like she normally does.

The boys seem to like me, either for me being me, or because I'm Cat's sister. The surfaces in the ultra-modern kitchen are very shiny, and they act like mirrors, so that I see Cat and then me. She's still half the size of me. Normally she's covered in layers so that you can't see her, just with her sparrow legs sticking out, but tonight she's in fitted top, body-con skirt and tights. She looks amazing. She sees me looking and smiles again. But this time the edge is there. I begin to feel I've outlived my welcome. My turn as a jester has come and gone and it's time to move on.

"I'm looking for Hannah," I say as I edge out, but no one looks as I go. I'm invisible again.

I've done the hall, kitchen and both downstairs rooms. I'm beginning to feel a bit down now. I could go back into the dance room and find a boy. But I'm not quite up for that. There's one boy in particular who's all I'm interested in.

I need a more chilled vibe for a while so I find my way through the French doors into the garden.

The cool air hits me and instantly I relax. It's beautiful out here, though I can barely see where I'm going in the dusk. I can just pick out a white lounger and aim for that. I stretch out on it, kick back and try to pick out how many colours there are in the summer evening sky. The sun's long gone but what remains is pale green and yellow, melting into ever deepening shades of blue. I wish Hannah were here to help me name all the colours.

"Having a good time?" A voice comes out of the darkness. I peer forward. A guy slumps down on the lounger next to me.

Be still my beating heart.

It's Matt.

"Great," I say, "but I need a minute to cool down. It's too hot in there."

"Yeah," he says companionably and then starts to roll something that looks suspiciously like a spliff. "Sending any more teachers over the edge recently?"

We chat for a time about things that annoy him at his school. The teachers who can't control the boys properly, who set work and don't mark it, the ones who clearly don't actually know what they are doing, the English teacher who can't spell or punctuate. There is banter; this feels good. We don't talk about *that* photo. It's like it never happened.

He hands me a spliff. I don't know what to do. Despite

Granny, I hate smoke. I hate drugs. I could say no. But then he might think I'm sad. And tonight of all nights, I want him to think that I'm cool.

I stretch my arm out for it but can't quite reach and, as I sit up and edge on to the side of the lounger, I find him sitting close to me and putting the spliff in my hand. I take it from him, our fingers meet. I can feel the warmth of his leg next to mine, and his hand now sits partially on my thigh. His shoulder presses on mine.

I pick out stars. I think I start to talk about them. He still sits close to me and seems to be watching me closely. I stop talking and turn to him. He smiles and I see again exactly how perfect he is. He strokes some hair away that was falling over my face and seems to consider me closely. For a second, I think that the world has stopped. Then I remember to start breathing. No one wants to kiss a corpse. He leans in closer. I just sit, utterly unsure of myself.

"Matt, you idiot!" a voice booms through the dark as some mountain of a boy lurches through the shadows towards us.

"Here you are," he shouts. "I've got him!" he calls back to the house. He stares cheerfully at us both, while a few others start to filter out, to sit down and chat. I don't know any of them, and Matt doesn't introduce me or look at me.

I get up from the lounger, unnoticed, and go inside, invisible again. The spotlight has moved on.

In the huge, modern bathroom, I lock the door and take a minute to compose myself. As I stare at my reflection in the mirror, I can barely focus on myself. Is that me in the reflection, behind all that make-up? In my head, there's a clip going round and round of Matt's face, his lips – only millimetres from mine in the soft midsummer dusk. And then his friend calls out and he acts as if I'm not there. If I could just get him to look at me again, then maybe I'd have a chance.

For a moment, I wonder whether I'm going to be sick and, indeed, whether I *should* be sick. I drink as much water as I can manage and then there's someone pounding on the door. I open it and some guy runs in and spews in the bath.

I go back into the main room. Izzie is now talking to Alex. She sees me and smiles joyously. I give her the thumbs up and wander on. After a while, I slip off. I have to see Matt. It's getting late and I can feel my time running out. I've no reason to see him after this, no reason to call round. I could message him but it's not the same.

He sat close to me – I could breathe in his breath.

Back in the garden, there are just chilled bodies. I see one of the guys I was talking to earlier. "Have you seen Matt?" I ask. He shakes his head.

But then the conversation turns and my attention goes back to Matt.

Back in the house, I can't find him anywhere. I stand at the top landing, wondering whether I can look upstairs or not. I see his tall shape at the bottom of the stairs, wine glass in hand. Garden guy walks past: "Matt, dude, how's it going?"

"Looking up, man, looking up."

"How so? Hey – that girl was looking for you."

"Which one?"

"You dog! You know – the fat one, Cat's sister?"

"Fat Girl? She's cool. But Zara's waiting for me and I think it would be rude to keep a lady waiting." With this, he jumps up from stair to stair. I push back behind some cupboard. He bounds past, his eyes flicker in my direction but he doesn't see me. A door opens, and framed in the doorway is Zara, smiling, a large shirt hanging off her, showing her bare shoulder and long, thin legs. She backs in, Matt follows her, the door slams shut.

I'm invisible.

Chapter 21

Jess Observation № 6: There are the things that you know you know. And the things that you don't. And then there are the things that you suddenly realise you knew all along, but never admitted to yourself till now.

I slump to the ground. My heart lies torn in rags. The words ring around me, burning in the air. *The fat one, Cat's fat sister, Fat Girl. Zara's waiting for me.* Upstairs now, his hands are on skinny Zara, his lips on hers. And I am crying in a corner, feeling fatter than I've ever felt before.

I feel someone sitting down next to me. Someone gives me a tissue. I look up. It's Alex. He doesn't smile or look at me. He just sits there.

"Thanks," I say.

He nods; we continue sitting like this.

"I'm not really having a great time," I say.

He nods again and goes off. *Oh well,* I think. *At least he looked at me.* I can't think what to do next. I look at my phone. I'm way past my curfew. There are several phone messages from Mum or Dad. I'm in deep doo-doo. I just sit there. I don't think that I can even walk home at the moment.

A heavy tread on the stairs. Alex again, with a glass of water. I drink it, I say thank you. He still doesn't look at me but I take the chance to look at him. He has Hannah's dark eyes but his hair is deep brown, not red, now that I look at him properly. He's tall and slim and, as I stare at him, I begin to see why Izzie would like him.

"Do you want to go home? Cos I'll take you if you do."

I nod. "But I need some fresh air first," I say.

He pulls me to my feet and pushes me up the stairs. I try to blank my mind about which room Matt is in at this time and exactly what he's doing to Zara or she's doing back to him.

Alex pushes open a door and pulls me through. I find my-self on some rooftop balcony, complete with seats and pot plants. We are high up, higher than the tall trees in the garden and the street. The sky is inky black now, but stained in the distance with the orange lights of central Manchester.

I sit down on a chair and Alex pulls one close to me.

I don't feel the need to make conversation, I just sit and stare. Some stars seem to be changing colour and jumping around a bit. A cool breeze hits us, I shiver but I'm glad. The whole evening, week, two weeks, have been overheated, and it's good to feel cold. It feels real.

"He's my friend, but he can be an idiot," Alex says simply. "I didn't know that you liked him. I would have said some-thing if I had." There is a pause. "You're not his type."

I nod, I don't question what this means. I don't need to be told the subtext. He doesn't go with fat girls.

The breeze, the water, the sudden peace – all begin to calm me down. Maybe I'm *too* calm. Maybe I'll break down when I'm on my own. Maybe I can just bounce back – I'm a fat girl after all, bouncy old me – and dust myself off and go back to being feisty Jess, good for a chat and a snog. But too embar-rassing to actually go out with.

It's too late now. The hot tears begin to slide down my cheeks. I don't shake or sob but I can't stop them, I know my make-up will follow their course, but I can't stop them.

Alex puts his hand on mine. I don't stop crying and I don't respond. Then he puts his arm round my shoulders and pulls me close. It feels good, his warmth and strength. My tears fall on his hand and he doesn't wipe them away. We stay like this for some time.

I've known him all my life and he's never been anything but kind and funny to me. And he's here now and he's not leaving me. I look up at him. He stares at me, and wipes away a tear from my cheek. My make-up leaves a black stain on his finger.

"I'm a mess," I whisper. He says nothing but leans in to kiss me. I pause for a slight second and then I kiss him back. It's soft, gentle and hot, all at the same time.

A door slams. I jump up, startled.

"Bitch," Izzie says, as she takes it all in with wide eyes.

"You bitch," she says again, with venom and tears beginning to form.

I reach out. "Izzie," I cry, but it's too late.

She's gone.

"What's that about?" Alex says, close behind me. Everything that I've forgotten about this evening, everything that I was blind to – too stoned, too drunk, too sad to remember – comes flooding back. Izzie came to the party feeling about Alex the way I feel – *felt* – about Matt. And what I feel about Zara, Izzie now feels about me. She's my best friend and I've betrayed her. The pit of my stomach goes cold.

I start after her, but Alex has me by the arm.

I try to shake him off, but he's insistent.

"Tell me what just happened here, because I'm all confused," he says.

I wipe tears from my eyes, the black make-up now leaving sad stains on the back of my hand.

"Izzie likes you," I say simply. "So that shouldn't have just happened."

"Oh," he says.

"Oh," I reply.

"I didn't know," Alex says, sadly. "I missed that." He looks at me intently. "I was just looking at you."

"I missed that too," I say, just as sadly.

"So," Alex says, "where does that leave us?"

"I don't think there is an us," I reply. "I've messed everything up in the last few weeks. I couldn't have got things more wrong if I'd tried."

I stop, because saying all of this is making me really sad. Alex. Liking me. For ages. If only I'd known. But then would it have made any difference?

"So I have to put it right with Izzie."

"I understand."

"I'm going to find her now."

"I'll help you."

So we go downstairs. The house seems empty now. The music still pounds out, making the floors and walls shake. Couples are here and there, strewn about like litter at the end of a festival. All the bedroom doors are shut. I search all the rooms downstairs but there's no sign of Izzie anywhere.

Alex goes to check the main room, where quite a few people still congregate. He comes back in a minute, shaking his head. Hannah is just behind him.

"What's up?" she says. "I've not seen you for hours. What's been going on?"

"Nothing," I snap. I don't want to explain anything. Then she'll know what a bad friend I am too and she'll side with Izzie.

"Where's Izzie?" she asks.

Alex takes over. "We're not sure. I think she's gone outside. We're going to find her."

"I'll come with you – give me a minute. But, Jess," Hannah says, "have you heard about Jack?"

"What?" I ask.

"He just turned up with another girl, his exgirlfriend, and dumped Cat in front of a whole crowd of people."

Confusion and frustration fizzes up inside me. Poor Cat. But I need to find Izzie. Now. I'd like to help Cat but I know that the last person she would ever turn to is me. Whereas I might have a chance to put things right with my friend.

"I'm not waiting," I say, opening the front door and walking down the steps.

Alex looks torn. "She'll just be—"

I spin round and look up at him. "I'm going. Now. If you want to wait, then wait. But you'll be doing it on your own." Then I start to walk as quickly as I can down the dark street, fumbling at my phone as I do so, trying to find Izzie's number.

Alex trails after me.

Izzie's number rings and rings but she doesn't answer it.

Then my phone flashes in the darkness. It's Izzie's number. I could cry with relief.

I read the message.

Curse you, Jess. Curse you. I will never forgive you.

"What is it?" Alex comes running up to me.

I burst into tears. "I just want to go home."

"Okay, then," he says gently, putting an arm round my shoulder. "Let's go."

And we walk home, and I'm glad he's there.

Chapter 22

Jess Observation № 7: Girls moan about magazines that make them feel bad about their bodies. Then they slag off every other girl's body. Girls, get a grip and start being a bit nicer to yourselves and everyone else.

We're home in minutes. I fumble when I get my keys out, though I'm feeling cold sober now. Alex puts his hand out to help me and we end up sort of holding hands.

He moves in as if for a kiss. But I can't. Not now.

I turn my head to the side and finally open the door. As I stand in the doorway and turn to say goodnight, he looks so sad that part of me wants to hug him. But it's too late and I'm too tired.

He shifts uneasily and flicks his long hair back out of his eyes. "I'm going back to find Hannah," he says. "I should have waited for her anyway."

"Okay," I say. "I'll text you tomorrow."

He nods, I nod. He begins to walk off into the light drizzle. I shut the door.

Dad is still up, strumming a few chords, sitting in a haze of smoke.

"All right, baby?"

"All right, Dad," I lie. "I'm off to bed." Tears are welling up but I just manage to keep them under control.

"Smart," he says and then drifts back into his happy little jamming session. I look back at him through the doorway, willing him to look back up, cos just now I need someone to look after me. Part of me just wants to burst into tears and cuddle up to him, tell him all about it, so he can make it all right.

But then he'd know what a bad friend I am.

And what a fool I've been.

And then he might look at me with disappointment. I don't think I could bear that. Anyway, no one can make this all right.

So I'm on my own. In my room the tears start falling, hot and wet. I want to take this bloody dress off but the zip's stuck. My fingers fumble as I try to get a good hold on it, but I'm tired and drunk and I can't do it.

All the thoughts that I normally manage to ignore overwhelm me. It's like Zara's in my head, looking so thin and perfect, telling me everything that's wrong with me.

Stupid, fat Jess, so fat that the zip on your dress is stuck. LMFAO

Finally, the zip moves and I rip the dress off, throwing it on the floor. It lies there, a symbol of all that's gone wrong tonight. All that preparation, all that hope . . . I think bitterly of how excited I was only a few hours ago.

What were you thinking? A girl like you, and Matt? Guys like that don't go for fat *girls. Because you can lose a few pounds, Jess, but you're still* fat.

I think about the last few weeks, and how rubbish they have been. All the headaches, stomach aches, the bad moods, the constant hunger: all for a door to open, for Matt to walk past me towards Zara's smiling face.

You think you're so smart, don't you Jess. You think you're different, superior to us normal girls. Well, look where it got you. Nowhere. Grow up. You'll never be anyone, looking the way you do. Face it, you've got life wrong – you and your crazy gran. Girls are judged on the way they look, and you fail on every level.

I lie, curled on my bed, trying to stop thinking, trying to stop replaying the evening over and over again.

"Cat's fat sister . . ."

And you dared to dream that something would happen between you and Matt. Well, I'm with him now. Right now, this second. It's me he wants, not Loser Jess.

And I know she's right. Right at this moment, I hate my body. It could have been me Matt kissed. It could have been me, now, with him. Matt liked me, he did, but I can't compete with girls who look like Zara. They might be shallow, they might be mean. But they're hot. And I most definitely am not.

I'm a fat, loser freak. Who has just got everything wrong.

And it's no consolation that Alex seems to like me. I mean, what was that?

He felt sorry for you, that's all. And anyway . . . Alex? I'm mean, he's not exactly gonna be in a boy band, is he? And you've never even looked at him twice in all the time you've known him. And when you did kiss him, you betrayed your friend. All this time you've looked down on me, but you're the backstabber. Izzie poured her heart out to you and you just ignored it.

Some friend you are, Jess Jones.

Now all I can see is Izzie's face, hard with anger, her eyes blazing at me. I've always prided myself on being one of the good guys in life. But I've behaved worse than anyone.

"*Curse you, Jess.*"

I'm a fat, loser freak. I sob into my pillow, pulling the duvet over my head, as if somehow this will protect me from the outside world.

But how can I protect me from myself?

The sky is light by the time I drift off into uneasy sleep.

When I wake up in the morning I feel like I *have* been cursed. But worse. My heart is broken.

I know it's a bit of a cliché. I never thought that it really happened – that your heart feels real pain. I thought it was just a metaphor. But no, it's true. My chest actually hurts, like there's physical damage in there. The tears start running down my cheeks again. There doesn't seem to be much point in wiping them away cos more just seem to replace them. I thought I might feel better in the morning. Well, I don't.

My phone beeps, but I don't want to see anything on it. Unless . . . Unless . . . it's Izzie.

I pick up my phone but it's not. It's Alex. I can't talk to him. I want to, but I don't think I can. Until I've worked out this mess of emotion that's inside me.

I try to make a start on sorting out my thoughts and feelings.

Okay, so I tried to be a "perfect" girl, whatever that is, for a while. I made myself lose weight for a guy. For three weeks I starved myself, I had the makeover, the dress. I did look different. And for what? I'm now more miserable than I have ever been in my life.

So either being perfect isn't for me, or being perfect isn't what it's made out to be.

And how does that leave me feeling about Matt? The bruise in my chest throbs particularly intensely at the thought of him. Yesterday I would have lain down in a puddle and let him walk over me. And now . . . And now . . . He's the kind of guy who chooses Zara over me.

I might have been able to cope with not getting off with him. I knew that was always likely to stay a fantasy. But I'm not coping well with him choosing Zara. Then I remember how he said that I'd got her wrong and that there was more to her than being a cow. I don't think my brain can cope with a world where I'm the bad guy and maybe Zara's okay.

Then I think about Cat. For the first time in a while we actually have something in common. Both of us had a bad night due to boys. But I didn't go and see if she was all right. I put Izzie first. That makes me a bad friend *and* a bad sister. Yet even if I had gone to find her, she'd probably have just given me that blank stare. Cos that's the way with Cat. Named after a cat; behaves like a cat. She walks on her own.

I wonder if my body can cope with a visit to Cat's lair, or if I'll get my face scratched. It seems stupid to me to have two of us in the house, heartbroken, and not talk to each other. But Cat's hardly spoken to me for a year – why would today be any different? I don't know who else to turn to. And she's my sister. That means something, doesn't it?

I drag myself out of bed. I can stand sort of steadily now and the room has stopped spinning. The mirror stands opposite me but I can't bear to look in it.

I walk the few steps across the landing from my room to Cat's. Why do I feel that I'm making the most enormous journey? Why, in fact, am I feeling nervous . . . when all I'm doing is trying to talk to my own sister?

I knock on the door.

No reply.

I knock again. "Cat?"

Is there movement inside? I begin to wonder if she actually came home last night.

Now I'm getting worried.

"*Cat?*"

I push open the door. It's quiet and dark in here. I know what this room looks like, though I hardly ever go in. The familiar Audrey Hepburn posters on the wall. The copies of *Vogue* neatly piled on the table.

A small lump under the duvet reassures me that at least she's not gone missing.

"Cat?" I repeat.

The lump moves.

The lump makes some kind of noise.

I could retreat now. I mean, she's not properly awake yet. If someone had tried to wake me up an hour ago I would have happily smothered them.

But something makes me press on.

I take a few steps into the room.

"Go away."

"No."

I wait. Only silence.

"Are you okay?"

"No."

"Then I'm not going away."

I sit in the chair next to her bed and pick up a book and start to read.

The duvet peels itself back and Cat stares at me.

"What are you doing?" she asks.

"I just wanted to make sure that you're all right."

She looks at me hard. "I'm fine."

"I heard about Jack," I say.

She bristles. "I don't want to talk about it."

I feel my bottom lip start to wobble. "Well, anyway, *I'm* not fine."

"Oh."

Okay, so that has really confused her. We don't talk normally. As you can probably tell by how well this conversation is going.

"Do you want to know why?"

Just silence. I want to scream at her but I try and keep it all together.

"Cat, I don't know who to talk to. I'm such an idiot."

"I could have told you that." There might be a hint of a smile on her lips.

"Don't be mean."

"Are you crying?" she says in surprise.

"Yes," I say, wiping away the tears.

"Oh." There you go – Cat, queen of the monosyllable.

"Is that all you can say?"

Cat leans back in bed. "Why don't you go and eat something, Jess? That's what you normally do when you're upset."

Ouch. That really hurts. "That's not fair," I reply.

She purses her lips into her usual pout. "Might not be fair, but it would be true."

At that point, our friend Silence fills the room again.

I'm the first to break it. "Can I ask you one question?"

"Okay."

I steel myself. We never talk about important stuff and I'm not sure how she will react. "Are you hungry all the time?"

After a short pause, she answers. "Yes."

"And doesn't that drive you mad?"

A cold smile crosses her face. "Yes."

"Then why do you do it?"

There is a longer pause now, but she's not chucked me out yet.

"Because I looked in the mirror and I didn't like the way I looked. So I did something about it."

"And now?"

"I still hate what I look like."

"But you're so pretty! Everyone thinks so!"

"My nose – I hate the shape of my nose. And my forehead – it's so big."

I stare at my sister's perfect face, even just woken up. She's so lucky to look in the mirror and see that.

But she's off now. I've never heard her speak so much and with so much feeling. She's listing all these minor imperfections with her face, her body: her freckles, the moles on her arms, the slight bump on her nose, her wonky eyebrows – it's like she's possessed.

"But Cat, you're beautiful."

She laughs hollowly. "But then why did Jack dump me? I

did everything for him. I read the magazines he liked, dressed the way he wanted me to, listened to the music he liked. Everything for him. And then he just dumps me like rubbish. Two-times on me with his ex. In public."

She pauses.

"That wouldn't have happened if I was perfect. Maybe I'm not the perfect person. But I can look perfect. That's the deal, isn't it – a girl has to look perfect and then everything else will be all right?" She looks almost desperate now.

"I tried being perfect for a bit but I don't think it's going to work for me," I say sadly. "I don't think perfect exists. And even if it does then I don't think it solves stuff."

I tell her about Matt, Alex and Izzie.

"Well, what did you expect? You set your sights too high! Matt and you . . ." Cat seems amused by all of this. "Now I get what's been going on." She considers what I've said for a moment. "Alex is pretty cool. He's not hot. You could do worse. I mean, it's about time you had a proper boyfriend."

"But I can't."

"Why not?"

"Izzie."

She looks at me as if I'm mad. "You'll need to get a new best friend."

At this point, I realise that Cat doesn't really have that many good girlfriends.

"I can't. She's my friend."

Cat makes that face again to show that she thinks I'm talking rubbish. I hear her stomach growl.

"Let me make you some lunch, Cat. I'll make you whatever you like."

She scowls. "Food. You think food is the answer to everything. I know you think I'm hung up about food, but so are you – just in a different way."

I'm about to argue with her. But then I think that maybe she does have a point. We *are* both hung up on food. She won't eat it and, left to my own devices, I can't stop.

"Maybe. But you need to eat."

She considers this. "I suppose so. I'll work it off later. Will you make me lemon and thyme chicken?"

I nod. "I'd love to."

"On one condition . . ."

I sigh. "Okay, what is it?"

"You work out with me later." She's smiling at me now. She clearly thinks this is hilarious. I don't.

"Cat, I'm hungover and heartbroken. Exercise is not going to help."

"No workout, no food."

I huff, "Fine. I'll do it." I mean, today can't get any worse.

"Great," she says. And this time she smiles at me as if she means it.

Actually, today has just got a little bit better.

Chapter 23

Invisible Rule № 16: Girls are supposed to show more emotion than they feel; boys are supposed to hide all the emotion that they feel.

The rest of the day is a strange mixture of misery and good stuff. I cook lunch for everyone, which is a miracle given how bad I feel. Dad, Mum, Lauren, Cat and I all eat together, sending up Gran a big portion. Then we watch *Doctor Who* box sets all afternoon. And it's nice. I mean, I don't stop thinking about the party, but it's hard to be too down with Lauren using your hair to hide behind every time something scary happens.

Then Cat makes me go running. And that is kind of miserable. I mean, you try running with a head that's being hit from the inside with a hammer while at the same time your stomach's churning with acid. Then add in a broken heart. But it's so miserable, it starts to be funny. And Cat and I find ourselves laughing together. Weird.

And that's that.

But nothing else is okay. TBH, when the day's over I don't sleep that well. There's a whole world whirling around in my head. At least I'm not hungry. But now I'm wondering if Cat was right. Is my obsession with food just the reverse of her decision not to eat? I think this over and over as the sky outside my window starts to brighten. A new day means another day at school. A day where I'll see Izzie . . . I feel sick.

I stay in bed as long as is humanly possible.

Mum stands outside my room and hollers repeatedly.

Then the door shuffles open and small footsteps whisper over the floor.

Mum's played her key card – Lauren.

The light blazes on.

"I can't see you," Lauren says.

"Turn off the light," I say, "it hurts my eyes."

"You should go to the doctor's then," she says, "you're not normal."

I pull the duvet over my head.

"You're damn right there, squirt," I mutter.

Like a trained torturer, she rips the duvet back. She's four – how did she learn all this?

"I am not a squirt. I am not water. I am a child."

"You are annoying," I say.

Her bottom lip sticks out and it starts to quiver.

"You don't love me," she states.

"Not when you wake me up like this I don't."

Tears start to roll down her cheeks. "Alice doesn't love me, and now you."

I can't take any more. "Okay," I say, "I give in." I sit up. I mean, I'm not going to sleep now am I?

And with that, she leads me downstairs as she shouts in triumph, "I got her up! Can I have my chocolate buttons now?"

I almost smile. My little sister has been used as a weapon against me by my mother, and she's traded me in for chocolate. That's my girl. I almost feel proud.

I'm about to launch into a tirade against Mum's underhand tactics, when I see an unexpected someone sitting at the kitchen table, eating. Someone who normally is not seen at breakfast time in our house. I bite back some kind of witty comment.

I settle for, "Hi Cat."

She nods at me as she cuts up very small pieces of fruit salad and delicately nibbles on one. Mum is standing behind her, drinking espresso, looking extremely pleased with herself. Daughter One eating breakfast, Daughter Two out of bed, Daughter Three being useful.

I think about what to eat. And I think about being tactful. And I think about what Cat said to me yesterday and how good it felt when we all got on.

"Any more fruit going?" I ask.

She pushes a large bowl towards me. "Knock yourself out."

So I dollop out the fruit – it smells great – and pour a reasonably generous amount of yogurt on top. With a bit of muesli for texture, it's not such a bad breakfast really.

Cat looks at my bowl and gives it the faintest Cat approval through the slight uplift in one perfectly groomed eyebrow.

TBH, this breakfast is really, really nice. And makes me feel a bit better.

Shower, uniform, bag, door.

I'm on the way to school. Hannah is waiting for me at the corner.

"Izzie told me what happened," Hannah says. "I don't think that she'll ever forgive you."

"I know."

She shakes her head. "You and Izzie, falling out over my brother. Now that is just stupid. I mean, his feet smell and he leaves hair in the shower. You really want to fight over that?"

I smile. "After the last few days I'm thinking of becoming a lesbian. I'm beginning to think that boys are too much trouble."

Hannah laughs. "You think so? I don't think girls are that perfect either. Girls would just argue over who would wear the best shoes. Anyway, count me out – I'm not going to snog you!"

And with that, she slings her school bag over her shoulder and together we face the day ahead. We walk slowly to school. My heart is hammering at the prospect of seeing Izzie. What can I say? What can I do to make everything back the way it was?

Just as I head up the slight hill which leads to school, I see a familiar slim figure ahead, with her skull and crossbones bag slung across her back. A bag that I bought for her cos I knew she'd love it. Has Izzie forgotten that I bought it for her, or is the fact that she's still wearing it a sign that she might forgive me? I wonder, as I run to catch up with her.

"Izzie," I call as I slow down next to her, panting after my jog.

She keeps on walking.

"I'm sorry," I try, the words tumbling over themselves as I attempt to get her to look at me.

She keeps on walking. Her eyes are fixed on some distant point.

"I'd change it if I could but I can't. You just have to know that I'm really, really sorry." Now my eyes are burning with red-hot tears.

She keeps on walking, no sign of any change in her face.

Suddenly, viciously, Izzie wheels towards me and stops. "Don't you dare talk to me. I didn't laugh at you when you said you liked Matt. I didn't say, 'No Jess, don't make a fool out of yourself, you're way out of his league.' No, I listened to you. I told you how I felt, how Alex made me feel. But the second my back was turned, you just helped yourself to him. Some kind of friend you are! Now keep away from me!" she snarls, and turns to walk up the road again.

Then she turns back and, for a second, I almost thank God. Has she softened?

"You keep away from me, Jesobel Jones. Because I'm going to make you pay for what you've done. And don't think that I can't, cos you know that I can." With that, she's gone. And I'm left standing on my own, on a pavement studded with turds, wondering just how much crap a girl can take in any one day.

Apparently just a bit more. Hannah, who has been hanging back, scoots past me.

"Izzie, wait up!" she calls.

"What?" I say, bemused.

Hannah turns back. "I'm just going to make sure she's okay."

This hurts. "But what about . . ." I begin, but Hannah is halfway to catching up with Izzie. She turns and yells back, "I'll see you later."

"But . . ." I think I'm starting to whimper. She's just chosen sides . . . and I'm the last in line, just like when we're choosing for netball.

F

M

L

That's all I've got to say.

Chapter 24

Invisible Rule № 17: Girls must never be on their own. Ever. It's against the law.

So there I am.

All on my own.

Walking to school.

Billy no mates.

This is not the look I wanted today. I mean, has no one noticed that my heart was broken yesterday? But then perhaps I haven't told anyone? I'm keeping this to myself cos I'm not sure what sympathy I'm going to get. As Cat said, "Well, what did you expect?"

So I sigh and trudge up the hill, thinking of how I can get Izzie to be my friend again.

My phone pings. A text from Alex. I want to open it, but is even that an act of treachery?

My fingers hover over the keys. Izzie won't know if I open it, will she?

All I'm doing is looking at it.

But then I don't look.

Because then I might be tempted to text back.

Not because I like him or anything.

But he was nice to me.

And that kiss was really, really nice too.

And not many nice things have happened to me lately.

In fact, the only good thing that's happened at all is that kiss.

But the kiss is also bad, bad, bad. Because Izzie likes him. And I don't want her to hate me.

School looms over me and swallows me up.

My day doesn't really get any better.

Form period spent with Hannah and Izzie huddled in a

corner, and me sitting in the Loser Corner on my own. Hannah throws me the odd comforting look but it's clear to everyone that there's been a split in our three and I'm the one on the outside.

Bex shuffles up to me and hisses, "What happened?" but I just shake my head. I don't know where to start and it all makes me too sad for words.

After a few lessons, where the teachers cram as much knowledge as they can into our already stuffed brains, I decide to go outside. It's actually a lovely sunny day. And I think sitting in the sun for ten minutes might just perk me up.

And it sort of does. There's a little shady bit on the far edge of the playing fields where there are a few big trees. If you lie back on a sunny day and watch the leaves dance in the sunlight, it's quite pretty. Okay, okay, I'm going a bit weird here I know but trust me, you should try it.

The peace doesn't last long.

The distant sound of nasal voices pierces my calm, accompanied by the sound of designer-clad feet.

Just what I need – Zara and her crew.

I don't open my eyes.

They plonk themselves a few feet away from me.

"Look at the text he sent me," Zara says, a bit too loudly, as though she wants me to hear.

"Oh how cute!" Tilly trills.

"God, he's so peng," Tara seconds.

"And you're actually going out now?" Tilly says.

I can hear Zara go on the defensive. "Of course! Look, my profile picture – it's us!"

They all shuffle round to peer at her phone. I don't need to look – it will be the latest mobile with unlimited credit. Only the best for her.

A note of triumph creeps into her voice. "And he's coming to the Prom with me? It couldn't get more perfect, could it? Matt and me at the Prom." Dramatic pause here. "I mean, imagine, how sad if you went to the Prom ON YOUR OWN. Imagine if you didn't take a boyfriend! How could you even hold your head up in public?"

I'm being provoked, I know.

I will respond. But not in the way that Zara expects.

I start with a very theatrical stretch and then roll over on to my tummy.

"Morning, all," I greet them with a very big, fake smile. "You had a good weekend then, Zara?"

She fixes me with her steely eyes.

"Yes, better than yours, I imagine. Did you know Matt and I got together at his party?"

I smile. "I think everyone between here and the North Pole knows that, Zara. Well done, I hope you both make each other very happy."

She stares at me, searching through my words for hidden meaning.

"No, seriously. Be happy, Zara!"

Her mouth opens but nothing comes out.

I look sincere. "I mean, it might be hard to keep up with Matt, won't it? You know, because he's really clever and seems to know about art and everything. But I'm sure you have lots in common."

Tilly butts in. "Well, I think that Zara can keep Matt happy in the way he cares most about at the moment, if you know what I mean." And she and the others burst out laughing. Apart from Zara, who is still staring at me.

"Sure," I say. "I mean, physical stuff is the basis for the start of a relationship. But then that might not be enough. I mean, when he wants to start discussing socialism and post-modernism and, well, any -ism you can think of, you're gonna have to have something to say, aren't you?"

Zara is staring at me. Her eyes are widening with what looks like rising panic.

"But that's cool, cos you know what all those things are, don't you?" I smile my sweetest smile. "Laters," I say, and amble off towards school and whatever scintillating lesson awaits me.

That might have been a bit mean. But it was fun. I can't believe that Matt really, really likes her. And the thought of her turning up with him to the Prom does hurt.

But there is nothing I can do about that.

And I think of what Granny would say. "A boy is just a boy.

He's not a sign that you've achieved anything. Not a possession." But it would be nice to have a boyfriend. Because I like being kissed and kissing back. Being held just feels so good. And while I know I shouldn't bother what other people think, it is nice to show the world that someone thinks you're fanciable and likes being with you enough to make that public to the world.

My phone pings again.

I look. Now it's four unread messages from Alex.

There's only so much that a girl can take.

I open the texts.

But at first glance, I have no idea what he's up to.

He's sent me four photos. And each one is of weirdly arranged food.

Well, not all of it. There's a close-up of a Polo mint. Then what looks like the letter K made out of breadsticks. A close-up of the R from the wrapper of a Rolo packet. And a U made out of peas. Yes, peas. K R U and . . . oh, the Polo is an O.

R U O K

I can't help but smile. I mean, he's the first person to ask me that all day.

As I head off to my next lesson, I think about what to text back.

But I can't do that.

Can I?

The rest of the day is like running on an educational treadmill, all hard work without actually going anywhere. I know I should think about all kind of GCSE-type things but all I can think about is what to say to Alex.

I walk home. On my own. I go and see Granny.

Through the fug of smoke in her room, I see her furiously sketching away. Her hands, wrinkly and knobbly, are still full of life.

I waft the smoke away and go and open a window. Granny just laughs at me. "Weed's medicinal. You should take full advantage of it."

"Gran, a few weeks ago you got me drunk and I ended up doing something stupid. So, no more narcotics from you."

Her eyes brighten up. "Tell your old Granny."

So, with a deep breath, I tell her about the photo I took of myself.

She laughs like a donkey.

"And then he sends you one back?"

"No, Granny, no. It's just something girls send to boys."

She snorts.

"Well, that's hardly fair. You've a beautiful body. Don't hide it away. But if boys expect you to do something and then won't do it themselves, then you need to think why. Next time, you ask for the photo of him first."

I look at the sketch Gran was just doing. The lines flow across the page and, from an apparent jumble of lines, a face emerges. Laughing. She's still got it. It's me. Only happy.

"And so, Jesobel, what's on your mind?"

I just tell her everything – about the party, about Alex, about Izzie.

She pulls long and hard on her roll-up, narrows her eyes and blows a long plume of smoke out.

"Friends are important. Many of my friends are dead now. But I still remember them. I still remember how they made me happy. But love. Love haunts you forever." She pauses. "Look into the mirror, Jess." She indicates a huge old mirror that hangs on the wall.

I shuffle around.

"Why?" I say, nervously.

"Because until you can see yourself in a mirror and like what you see, you have no business asking anyone to love you."

I don't look at myself in the mirror. I'm not sure who I'll see.

She leans back and fixes me with those fierce eyes.

"So if you're not ready for love yet, maybe sort things out with your friend."

That seems like good advice to me. But how? How do I get Izzie to talk to me?

I can only think of one way open to me.

I need to bake a cake.

Chapter 25

Jess Observation № 8: Being fat was once a sign of being rich;
being tanned a sign of being poor. I live in the wrong time!

With great care, I slowly climb down the bus steps and stand on a verge, trying not to look as lost and confused as I feel.

I feel like I've come much further than a thirty-minute bus journey. Where me and Hannah live it's all big houses, tree-lined streets and delis selling quinoa and linseed (both foods of the devil if you ask me. Mum says that they improve your life expectancy. I'd rather eat jam and scones and die young). Here the houses are smaller, scruffier, and the only shop I can see sells cheap alcohol. Which is obviously a plus. But I can't help but feel that I don't belong here.

I would get my phone out to check where I'm going but I daren't. The cake box takes both hands to carry and, after three hours' work, I can't bear to put it down even for a second, in case something terrible happens to it.

You might ask why I don't know the way to Izzie's house. I mean, you say, aren't you supposed to be best friends (apart from the bit where you snog the boy she fancies just cos the boy you fancied has gone off with UberCow from Hell)?

Well, I would answer, smarty pants, that she only moved here a year ago. And she's never invited us round. She always comes to us. And I think I'm beginning to understand why.

I mean, it's not that it's horrible or anything. Just different. I mean, I can't say I'm better than anyone cos I live in a big house. Gran's house. Mum and Dad have never done anything to make enough money to buy a house. They're just very good at spending it. On themselves. And clothes that don't fit me.

But I am getting a few looks now, mainly, I guess, cos I'm just standing here with a cake. Not moving. Which, regardless of which neighbourhood you live in, is pretty weird.

So I start to move, visualise the map I memorised on the bus, and try not to think about what Izzie is going to say when she sees me.

I think instead about the cake. I have tried very, very hard with the cake. It's Victoria sponge with blackcurrant jam in the middle, which is her favourite. Then a covering of royal icing. So nothing special there. But what I have tried really, really hard at is the decoration. I've created replica tarot cards in gingerbread and icing and made them into a tower. Which is why I'm carrying the cake so carefully. On the top is the Fool. I hope that she sees that that is me. And you might be thinking, Why am I doing this? Well, she won't answer my texts or my calls or my emails. I just don't know what else to do.

I find the right road, I count down to the right house. A small semi, clean and tidy. The kids who cycle round on choppers look pretty much the same as the kids who skateboard round where I live, only the labels on their clothes are different.

I ring the doorbell.

And wait.

And wait a bit longer.

My arms are hurting from carrying this bloody thing. I think I might drop it soon. It seemed like a good idea at the time.

The door opens.

Izzie stands there, taking in the scene. I check her face to see if there's even a whisper of a smile anywhere to see me standing there with a very large cake.

No.

Nada.

Not one iota of welcome there.

You're gonna have to try harder this time, Jess.

But she doesn't shut the door straight away.

I decide that the straight-out apology might not be such a good approach. I mean, she's ignored all my many attempts at saying sorry so far so I don't see what's going to be so different this time.

"Izzie," I say. "Any chance that you might be hungry?"

"Not really," she says. "So I think you've had a wasted trip."

"Can I come in?" I say. "Just to drop this off. You might be hungry later." I smile as warmly as I can. "My arms are killing me, Iz."

She's wavering, I know. She's a nice girl. She doesn't really want to slam the door in my face, but then a bit of her still does.

"I made it especially for you."

"I didn't ask you to. I just want you to leave me alone."

"I know. Izzie, I know. I know that I've really messed up. If I could take it back then I would. I would do anything, anything to make things right with you, I really would. But I can't change what I did. All I can do is hope that at some point you might forgive me."

I think I'm about to drop the cake. I mean, every muscle is burning in my arms, trying not to drop it. Why didn't I think about the practicalities of transporting a huge, decorated sponge on a bus and then walking? "Izzie, I'm going to have to . . ."

Her face darkens. "You, why is it all about you? It's just a bit weird, Jess. You mess up and you think you can just a bake a cake and smile and everything will just be back to normal. But you hurt me, Jess. And I'm not sure that I can forgive you."

The cake. My arms. Why didn't I do more arm exercises when I was into exercise? Why did I not have the ability to see into the future and go – *Yes, I need to build up my arm muscles for the day I need to carry a really, really big cake and my whole life will depend on it?*

"I know. Talking of things hurting – thing is, Izzie, my arms—"

"I don't care," she cries. "I don't care about you and I don't care about your bloody cake."

At this point, it starts to tip forward and while I try to stop it by twisting my hands back, it gains momentum. With a horrendous rush, the sponge, icing, jam and butter cream transforms from a work of art to a mush of wet crumbs on the doorstep.

We both look at it. Izzie is torn between anger and something else.

We look at each other. A bit of me wants to cry. "I know you're right. I know a cake won't fix anything. But it wasn't just a cake. I don't always have the right words. So it's my way of saying that you're my friend. And I miss you."

I can't deny that my voice wobbles at this last point. With my foot, I shove the icing Fool-card towards her so that she can see what I tried to do for her.

"Look," I said. "I really tried to make something you'd like. I copied the tarot cards that you gave me."

Izzie pushes her dark hair away from her face so she can see it better. "The Fool?" she says.

I nod.

"Now would that be you?" she says. "Or me, for thinking that you were my friend?"

With that she slams the door, leaving me standing in the street as the streetlights start to come on, surrounded by the broken remains of my cake. A skinny dog rushes up and starts to eat the crumbs. I walk away, I don't stop him. At least something, if not someone, will enjoy it.

The street turns a bit fuzzy at that point.

I blink away the tears, and retrace my steps to go home.

Chapter 26

Invisible Rule № 18: Everybody is supposed to look down on some-one else. Society just grinds to a halt otherwise.

I don't enjoy the bus journey home. I don't want to cry in public. But I just need to have a good sob. In the past, I've had the odd minor fall-out when we've not agreed over which is more powerful: crystals or cake. And that's it. And now, it's like nuclear fallout. And the worst thing is that there is abso-lutely nothing that I can do to sort it out. And I'm a teenager who goes to the world's most repressive school so I know a thing or two about being made to feel powerless.

I can't help it but I also think about Alex. I scroll through the texts from him and I smile. He seems to be the only person who really cares about me, but he's also the one person I can't talk to. Then I think: What if Izzie never forgives me? Then I'll have ignored the one person who seems to like me for no reason.

Then my crazy brain thinks about Cat. How she made me do exercise and I almost enjoyed it. Between the expert exer-cise guru and the master baker, surely there's some kind of amazing solution. There's a half formed plan in my mind. I just can't quite find it yet.

My phone buzzes. Alex. Only a few days ago, it was the letters *MATT* that got me all excited, but how things have changed. Alex has texted me before and I've never even thought about it twice. But now things are different.

I open it. It would be rude not to.

How do you avoid a soggy bottom?

I smile. I text back before I have a chance to think about it.

What are you making?

A chicken pie. Something manly. I'm making it for you.

You need to bake it blind.

WTF???

Oh dear. You have much to learn J.

I clearly need help. Any chance of a tutorial?

And then he sends a picture. Well, I can't help but LOLing. Which means some old dear on the bus gives me a dirty look. I know – give me an ASBO for enjoying myself. As I'm under eighteen obviously I'm on my way to rob a bank or something just because I'm having FUN.

In the photo is the worst excuse for a pie I've ever seen in my life. It's grey, with gravy seeping out from several gaping cracks on the top and it's broken down the side.

But he made it for me. And that's pretty damn cool.

Presentation seems to be an issue.

But taste is everything, isn't it?

I can't taste it in a photo.

True. You may never get to experience this one. Such a shame.

And I'm smiling. My face is splitting from side to side.

I keep tapping out messages and they keep coming back. I'm not sure where this is going, but I like it.

By the time the bus finally drifts back to my neighbourhood and the steely old granny has shuffled off into the night after giving me one last disapproving tut, I'm glowing. Yes, I can still see Izzie's angry face. But the last fifteen minutes have been fun. And it's what I needed.

I practically skip back home. My soul skips, anyway. My feet just walk in a more acceptably cool fashion. I like to be different, but there have to be limits.

Within a few minutes, I'm very glad that I kept my skipping under control. There's a tall figure standing opposite my house. Definitely male – tall and on the rather skinny side. He straightens up when he sees me and then smiles. And I think that if I *had* skipped up the road, I don't think he would have actually minded. Because I really think that he likes me. Not thinner, or smarter, or older, or more fashionable. I think he gets me, and still likes me.

"Hey," I say.

"Hey back," he says.

In his hands is a small plastic box. In the small plastic box is a small, grey pie. Alex regards the pie sadly.

"I won't ask you to try it," he says. "It's too embarrassing."

"It's okay," I say. "It might taste all right."

He shakes his head. "I wouldn't bet on it."

I take the box from him. His fingers and mine graze past each other. I can't help but remember how good it felt when he held me and how strong his hands felt. I daren't look up directly at him.

Instead, I poke the pie. I break a bit off and taste. I chew thoughtfully.

"It's very . . . manly," I say.

And then I start to choke, laughing.

"Seriously," I say when I can speak, "this is the most masculine pie I have ever tasted. I am almost overwhelmed by the maleness of this pie."

He makes a face. "The words 'masculine' and 'pie' just don't go together, do they?"

I eat another piece. "It's not bad. But you need to keep your hands cold when you're making the pastry. And don't mix it for so long next time." I chew and then nod. "Actually, it tastes okay. Is that cloves in the sauce?"

"Little smelly bits of wood?" he replies.

"That's the ones," I say. "I love cloves."

And then we stand there. Under the neon light, as the sky turns dark above us.

"I'd ask you in, but . . ."

"I know, it's getting late."

"No, it's not that. It's my mother. She'd probably just leap on you."

He smiles. "Yeah, I remember Jack telling me about her."

There's silence for a minute. I don't think now is the time to bring Jack into anything. I mean, that's ancient history. Neither do I really want to discuss my mum and her perfect boobs. And there's the unspoken thing that remains very obviously unspoken. Izzie.

Then I make a mistake. I look at him properly. I notice for the first time, as we stand in the neon light as the sky gets darker above us, that his eyes are really, really lovely. Like amber, flecked with gold. There is something incredibly sexy about a guy staring at you as if you are the most important thing in the world. Cos that's how I'm feeling right now. And it's the best thing I've ever felt. Better than food. Better than a laugh with my friends.

He puts his hand up to brush away some hair that's blown across my face. I don't move away. I just keep staring at him.

That's when we kiss. Again. And it's just as good as last time.

Then we stand there, in the shadows. And his hand, stroking through my hair, might just be my latest favourite thing.

We stand there for a bit longer. I wish I could stay here forever.

But I can't.

Finally, I pull away. "Night," is all I can croak out.

"Night," he says sadly. He watches me as I unlock the door and go inside. I peek out the window. He stands there for some time. And I keep watching until he goes.

Chapter 27

Invisible Rule № 19: Dads must drive at the weekend, even if mums are better drivers. Just like mums must do more housework even if they work longer hours. It is THE LAW.

I float up the stairs to my room.

I do not go to the kitchen. I do not have a snack before bed. I just waft up the stairs, shouting a happy goodnight to anyone I pass.

Mum, on the treadmill in the front room, looks at me with suspicion. "Are you all right, Jess?" she calls, with a note of caution in her voice.

"Just fine, Mother dear," I reply.

Now she looks really worried.

When I get to my room, my phone goes again. I just hope it's nothing bad.

Alex.

Sweet dreams.

Now I float and glow all at the same time. Cat peers round the door. I'm so caught up in the moment that I don't go, "Bloody hell, Cat, why have you actually stooped to enter my room? Are you okay?" But I don't think any of that because I am happy.

"What's wrong with you?" she says.

"Nothing. I am happy. Look. This expression on my face? It's called a smile. You ought to try it."

She scowls at me.

I respond, "Nope, you've got it all wrong. That's called looking like a mardy cow."

She starts to retreat and then I feel a bit bad. Now I think about the fact that she has not willingly entered my room for over a year and that perhaps I should be nice about that rather than tease her (though I am enjoying it just a bit).

"What's up, Cat?"

She mutters something like, "Six thirty. That's the deal."

I have no idea what she is talking about. You have to give it to Cat, she does do enigmatic pretty well.

So there we are. I'm still feeling dreamy. I just send Alex a smiley face. I mean, what more is there to say just at the moment?

And then I send a heart.

Then I worry that that might seem a bit pushy.

I mean, is that too much?

But then I think that a moment ago his lips were firmly on mine and his hands seemed quite interested in wandering about my body, so I'm not sure that he could really think, *Oh no, she's sent me a heart, that's showing too much commitment at this time.*

So I get ready for bed, and fall asleep with a smile on my face and my phone in my hand.

Until six thirty the next morning.

When Cat wakes me up. And makes me go for a run and then a workout that would make an Olympic athlete cry. I never knew I even had all the muscles that are now screaming with pain.

So by the time I get to school, I'm exhausted. I mean, I'm trying to prepare for my GCSEs, mend things with my sister and with Izzie, deal with the fallout from the whole party thing, keep away from supercow Zara, and make the odd cake while I'm at it. I don't have the energy to get fit.

Lesson One.

English. Izzie does English with me. I don't like to think about what she will or won't say when she sees me. But a bit of me is still upset about the cake. I mean I really, really tried. And she just rejected it. I know I'm in the wrong but I'm not sure what else there is I can do.

There's a seating plan and we can't sit where we like so I'm safe on that count. Until the dreaded words come, "Right, we're working in random groups today." Mrs Lewis picks out lolly sticks with people's names on them to make the groups.

I just know what is going to happen.

And then it does.

"So – Jess, Tilly, Rosie, Izzie. You're group three. Everyone get into their groups now."

Oh joy. I'm not sure I can take another hour of feeling completely and utterly rubbish. I think about Alex and me, warm in the shadows last night, and now I feel even worse. I don't quite look Izzie in the eye. She's not saying anything.

But she looks sad.

Not angry any more.

Just sad.

We look at the task in front of us.

Which character do you think is most to blame for the events in The Crucible?

Rosie looks vacant and pushes her glasses up and down. Izzie stares out of the window, Tilly checks her make-up in the glass of her phone and I don't say anything.

After a minute or two of this, the strain of not saying anything is nearly killing me. I mean, it's not exactly hard. If you don't know *The Crucible*, it's just some seriously messed up girls who pretend that they're witches a few hundred years ago cos they're bored. The rest of the villagers believe that they are witches and threaten to kill the girls. Then the girls go "Oops, okay, I was a witch, but now I'm not but I can tell you who the real witches are" and then they start accusing anyone they don't like of being witches. And cos the grown-ups believe them, those people end up getting executed. Yep, really. And some grown-ups think that kids are messed up – but they're the ones writing this stuff. And then getting us to learn all about it for exams.

Then Tilly sighs. "Well, if no one else is taking this seriously, I suppose I'll have to do all the work." She sniffs and looks at the rest of us with disdain.

She picks up the card with her perfectly manicured nails.

"So . . . who's to blame? It's got to be Elizabeth."

Rosie looks even more vacant. "Oh . . . yes . . . maybe."

I stare at Tilly until she goes, "What, Jess? At least I'm contributing. You're not doing anything. Or is that because the only topic that interests you is food?"

I ignore that bit.

"Elizabeth," I say. "Probably one of the only two decent

characters in the play, both of whom are women, by the way. Exactly what does she do wrong?"

Tilly looks at me with triumph.

"If she'd slept with her husband, then he wouldn't have had the affair with that girl, Abigail, and then *she* wouldn't have wanted Elizabeth dead and that would have been it. End of." She leans back and smirks.

Izzie is now showing some interest. I mean, she is actually looking at us rather than out of the window.

I'm on a roll, so I continue. "This is warped on so many levels. Elizabeth was *sick*, don't you get that? Might have been suffering from baby blues. Giving birth's not a doddle, you know – pushing out a watermelon through a drainpipe? So maybe she didn't feel like it for a bit. Don't you think that John might be at fault for not being able to keep his trousers zipped?" I don't draw Tilly's attention to the fact that they didn't use zips then, but I think my point remains valid.

Tilly looks at her planner with disgust. "If a girl can't keep a man, then she's only got herself to blame. She probably let herself go." She flicks me a sideways glance, exaggerated by those false black lashes of hers.

I feel myself getting angrier. I am sort of aware of Mrs Lewis paying more attention than she should to the group. "So he's not responsible at all? Cheats on his wife when she's ill, makes a girl love him and then dumps her in public?"

Tilly ignores this. "God, Jess, you're such a *feminist*. Live in the real world. A guy gets frustrated, then of course he's going to chase the first hot girl he sees. That's just life. Rosie, you think I'm right, don't you?" She turns confidently to cowering Rosie, who just trembles at the sheer horror of having to have any kind of firm opinion at all.

Then she focuses on Izzie. "Izzie, I know you and Jess aren't seeing eye to eye at the moment. And anyway, *you're* not going to turn on your fellow witches, are you? You agree with me, don't you, that Elizabeth is the one to blame here?"

By now the whole class is listening to us.

"This is good, girls – I've been listening. This is excellent," Mrs Lewis cheers us on. "Well, Izzie, who are you siding with – Tilly blaming Elizabeth or Jess blaming John?"

I start to protest that I've not blamed anyone. In fact I don't even like this task – it's way too judgemental for my liking.

I know what's coming though. I know Izzie will just side against me. But with Tilly, and in public? It's just too hard to bear.

"I think Jess is right."

I look at Izzie. She isn't looking back but she is looking at Tilly as if she were some kind of worm. That she might chop up and use in a potion.

For the second time in twelve hours, I feel happy.

Tilly tuts. "You would say that."

Izzie continues, "I blame the puritan culture that said anything fun was a sin; and the patriarchal culture that stopped young women from expressing themselves."

"Lesbian," Tilly whispers, so that Mrs Lewis can't hear.

Mrs Lewis beams. "We could discuss this all day. But we need to prepare for the exam now." And then she drones on about what we need to write next.

I try to catch Izzie's eye and smile at her. She shoots the shortest, briefest smile in my direction.

But it's enough.

It's a start.

I'm not getting too excited yet, but it's better than being ignored.

I get on with my rant against the evils of men who can't control their urges (though to be fair the guy who cheats on his wife does get hanged, which even I think is a bit harsh).

The lesson finally finishes and it's time for morning break. I think of what to say to Izzie. I mean, she broke the silence. Is the next step up to me?

We start to walk back to our form room. Are we walking together? I mean, we're walking in the same direction, at the same pace. But we're not talking. Do I need to say something? This is driving me mad.

"I'm—"

"Do you—"

We smile at each other, both talking at the same time. Triple hurray, she smiled at me!

"You first," I say. "I seem to have done a lot of talking lately and it's not done me much good."

"I'm sorry about the cake," Izzie says. "It must have taken you hours."

I nod. "It did. But I didn't mind. I know it was stupid and just a cake but I didn't know what else to do."

"Did you mean what you said last night?" Izzie asks. "When you said that you'd do anything?"

I nod. I did and I still do.

We're outside now and she goes to sit down on a scruffy bench. I follow her.

She takes a deep breath.

"The thing is, Jess, I miss you. I really do. And I want to be friends again. It's not the same without you. But it hurt me what you did."

I can only nod. I know.

"I want to be friends," she continues.

I breathe a sigh of relief.

"God, I'm so glad that you said that Izzie cos—"

She holds up a hand to stop me from talking.

"But there's one thing…"

I stop. What can she mean? I said I'd do anything, but Izzie's not the mean type. She's hardly about to ask me to do something horrendous.

"I just don't think I could bear it if you and Alex got together. So for us to be friends . . . I have to ask you to promise not to get involved with him. I just couldn't take it."

I look at her.

I think about what she's saying.

I think about how, only last week, all I could think of was Matt.

And all I've been able to think about today is Alex's lips on mine.

Alex – or Izzie?

Oh. But then I hear a voice speaking, and it's mine.

"Okay. No problem. I mean, that's never going to happen anyway." I smile at her. "So we're friends again then?"

She smiles back. "Friends."

Never, in the course of history, have I ever smiled such a fake smile.

Chapter 28

Jess Observation № 9: When it rains, guys can't use umbrellas or coats. Ever. Hoodies are okay. But just being seen with an umbrella could ruin a boy's reputation for life.

In fact, my face aches so much it hurts. Ever heard the saying *Be careful what you wish for*?

I wanted Izzie to forgive me. I said I'd do anything. And she called my bluff.

Hannah comes over and hugs us both. She's leaping with excitement, like a puppy with a new toy.

"God, I'm so relieved," she squeals. "I hated the last few days so much." She takes a long look at my face. "But now we're all back together again, aren't we?"

I smile my fake smile back. "Oh yes, everything's just tickely-boo."

She and Izzie both burst out laughing. "Only you say such stupid things, Jess." Hannah hugs me. Then Izzie does. So that means that Everything is A Okay.

So why do I feel so rubbish for the rest of the day? You'd think that I was used to it by now. I am glad Izzie is my friend. And I couldn't choose Alex over her because he's just a boy and I still don't know exactly how I feel about him.

In a way, I know why she asked me to promise that. Because if it were me, it would kill me to see my best friend and the guy I like together. In front of me. Kissing. Etc.

So I've chosen Izzie. Friendship first. Sisters stick together. I've always looked down on girls who dump their friends, their principles, their likes and dislikes, their knickers, for a boy. But now I get it. I'm not saying I'd do it. But I get it. Cos friends make you feel special in one way, but a boy can make you feel special in another way.

The only thing that bugs me now, and bugs me for the rest

of the day, is this. I'm not sure that I would have done what Izzie did. I'm not saying I'm a saint, cos it's clear that I'm not. But I don't think I'd have made Izzie promise what she's made me promise.

But I've made a commitment and I'll stick to it.

All this buzzes round my head all day, leaving me feeling a bit sick. If Izzie notices, she doesn't say anything. Hannah is too wise a soul to comment just yet. It's all those novels she reads that give her insight into the human psyche.

Finally, the last bell of the day goes and we shamble out of school. Just as we agree to go and get some frozen yogurt (Jeez, we live on the edge we do), my phone rings. I see I've had a number of texts/missed calls while I've been in lessons. Obvs my phone has been on silent. You don't want to get your phone confiscated – that's like having your human rights violated or your arm amputated. I mean, you don't exist without it, now, do you?

It's Mum.

Odd.

She doesn't normally ring me. Ever.

"Hi darling. I'm parked just next to the school. Can you come and find me?"

I share looks with Hannah and Izzie.

"Is everything okay?" Izzie asks.

"Maybe I should have got you to read my cards," I joke.

We say goodbye and I look for Mum's battered old BMW. It's all she can afford but she won't get rid of it cos of the logo. No Skoda or Ford for Mum. Even if it is twenty years old and starting to sag.

I get into the back.

"You're sitting on Alice," Lauren protests. "Move over, she hasn't got any room."

Reluctantly, I do. Cat is in the front seat, looking stony faced. Mum is in the driving seat. I'd say she's looking pale and drawn under the fake tan and the Botox but it's hard to tell.

"What's up?" I say.

"I'm sorry, love, it's Gran. She's been taken into hospital." And with that, she pulls out in front of a four-by-four, swears at the driver and races off.

I stare out the window in disbelief. Gran . . . ill. I feel like some rugby player has just landed a flying kick in my stomach.

During the course of the journey, I find out that Gran's cough was much worse today. Mum heard noises from upstairs and found Lauren shaking Gran, who was lying on the floor, wheezing.

"Alice said she was being lazy, but I said she was poorly. Her face was all grey and she sounded like Darth Vader," Lauren says without any obvious emotion.

My heart is thumping. I'm not sure I can take many Laurenisms today.

Mum says, "The ambulance came really quickly. Dad went with her. They put her on oxygen – the doctors will tell us more when we get to the hospital."

So we swerve through the traffic, Mum driving like a maniac, but for once it's not quick enough for me.

As we go, I think of Gran, plumed with smoke, with a glass of whisky in her hand. About how she gives me a drink from my special glass. Of the photo that she showed me. How she's always told me to be proud of myself, not to follow the crowd. And I think of how much she's part of me, part of our family.

As I think of her body lying on the floor, and how empty our house would feel without her, I can't stop the tears in my eyes.

Mum and Cat are silent apart from the odd swearword that Mum fires out to any driver in her way. It takes too long to get there, too long to find a parking space, too long to find the right ward through the labyrinth of corridors with their too-bright lights and antiseptic shine.

Eventually, we see a figure we know. Dad. Looking tired, even old, for a change. We all hug him in turn. He hugs us back.

"Well?" I ask.

He pauses for a moment. "We just need to wait and see."

"But what does that mean?" I persist. "Is she going to be okay or not?"

Dad doesn't answer. My words just hang in the air between us. Mum puts an arm round me and squeezes my shoulder.

Lauren puts a small hand in mine and snuggles into me.

"She's in the best place. They'll take very good care of her here," Mum says gently.

Dad gestures towards the door next to him. "She's in there. The doctors are with her now." His voice breaks as he speaks.

Tears slide down my face. I don't think I can cope with my dad crying.

"Hey now, no need for that, kiddo," Dad says, wiping away my tears and forcing his voice to become normal. "Don't mind your old man – it's just the shock. Your gran is a tough old bird."

I nod, still not able to speak. I look through the glass panel in the door. There's no sign of Gran – my view of the bed is blocked by hospital staff.

At this point, Lauren announces that she's hungry, so Mum takes her to find something to eat. Dad, Cat and I find some chairs to sit on and just wait.

After a while, the door opens and a young woman with a tired face and hair pulled back into a bun, comes over to us.

"Mr Jones?" she asks. Dad nods and she continues, "I'm Doctor Flanagan. I've been treating your mother this afternoon."

"How is she?" The words burst out of me.

"These are two of my daughters," Dad says to her as Doctor Flanagan continues to speak, this time including me and Cat in what she says.

"Your mother – your grandmother – has pneumonia. We're treating it with antibiotics, we've put her on a drip to help rehydrate her and we're also giving her oxygen through a tube, because she's not getting enough on her own."

"But she's going to be okay?" I ask. "I mean, pneumonia's not that serious, is it?"

Doctor Flanagan thinks before she speaks. This worries me.

"You're right, pneumonia is often easily treated. But it can be serious for some people. Especially the elderly."

What is she saying? I just want her to tell me that Granny's going to be fine. Why won't she just say it? Unless – unless . . . Granny is not going to be fine.

The doctor continues, "We're giving her the treatment she

needs and we'll assess the situation at every step." Which sounds reassuring, but it's really not.

Then she puts her hand on Dad's arm and takes him to one side, speaking to him in a quieter voice. I know she's doing this to stop me and Cat hearing but I get most of it. *Malnourished* is one word she uses. Then, *Poor lung condition.* And *I believe she lives with you* then *She's frail for her age.* So Granny is in here cos of us. *You need to prepare yourself.* We don't look after her well enough. I think of all the trays of food I take her. How rarely she eats anything. How no one challenges her about it. How Dad takes her up her tobacco and "special" cigarettes. *She might not make it through the night.* How her cough has got worse and worse and, again, not one of us has ever thought to suggest that she stop smoking or that we stop taking her what she asks for.

It's our fault. We love Granny. But we've let her down.

Dad comes back to us, trying to put a brave face on, but failing.

"So . . ." says Cat.

"So . . ." Dad replies, "Granny's tough. We just need to wait and see if she responds to treatment." He pauses, realises he's made a mistake. "*How* she responds to treatment is what I meant to say."

He's a terrible liar.

"So she might not make it," Cat says bluntly. "We heard most of what the doctor said. We're not deaf, we're not stupid and we're not children."

Dad doesn't look at us. "We just have to wait."

"I want to see her," I say. I push open the door and nervously enter the small room. It's quiet in there, apart from the regular electronic beeps from various monitors. In the middle of the room is a narrow bed. In it, lies a small body. I walk over. Granny. Her eyes are closed, a plastic tube is taped to her face.

I reach out for her hand. Her skin is like paper.

I can't hear her breathe. I lean over just to make sure. Like the distant sound of the sea, I can make out tiny, shallow breaths.

I squeeze her hand. "Hang on in there, Granny," I say out

loud. Inside, I repeat over and over again, *I'm not ready for you to go yet.*

But her hand rests, unresponsive, in mine. She doesn't squeeze back.

Chapter 29

Sometimes life is very, very sad. End of.

It's a long night.

Dad refuses to budge from Granny's side. He also refuses to let me and Cat stay. So Mum takes us home when visiting hours are finished. By now, Lauren is fast asleep in the back of the car with me.

Once home, Mum puts her to bed while Cat and I slump in the kitchen. Yet again, I don't feel much like cooking. But one look at Mum's face when she comes down and I know that I need to make an effort, so I start to make pasta. From scratch. Comfort food. But not just for me. For my family.

I lose myself for a time in the kneading, stretching and rolling. Cat asks to help so I get her to to start making pesto. I can't help but notice that she doesn't use enough oil but I figure now's not the time to start being picky.

So it's a tense sort of meal. Me, Mum and Cat. All picking at our food, all with our phones next to us, jumping each time any of them rings, beeps or buzzes.

Anytime Mum's phone rings, it's like an icy fist crushes my heart.

I know everyone dies someday. Hell, I know I'm gonna die someday. I know that Granny is old. But my first ever memory was with her. It can't be her time yet. Let's face it, most days she's the only grown-up who never lies to me, who's always there when I need her. And I still need her. Because who will I turn to if she's not there . . .?

My phone beeps. It's Alex. Hannah must have told him about Granny. It's a sweet text. *Hope you're okay. Thinking of you. Your gran rocks x*

An X. A cyber kiss. Not as good as a real one but still pretty special.

I think of Izzie and her ultimatum. I think of Gran lying in her hospital bed.

I don't know what to do.

What would Granny do? One of the last things she said to me was to sort things out with Izzie.

With clumsy fingers and a sinking heart, I text back. I tell him that things are difficult. That I'm going to be at the hospital lots. That it might be better if we forget about the other night. I don't put a kiss at the end. That might confuse.

I press send.

It's done now. I can't take it back.

My phone screen stays dark. He doesn't text back. Oh Izzie, I hope I've done the right thing.

It's late now. Cat pours Mum a large glass of red wine and a small one for me and her. It tastes like vinegar to me. We all leap in the air when Mum's phone goes.

"It's your father," she whispers. Cat and I stare at her, gauging her face for every emotion.

"She's stable," Mum says as she hangs up. "Your dad's staying with her. It's late, girls, you need to get to bed."

So we troop off. As Cat and I reach the landing, she turns to me. "I don't think I'm going to sleep well tonight," Cat says.

"Me neither."

"Do you want to sleep on the pull-out in my room?" Cat asks.

And as she says it, I realise that I want that more than anything.

"Okay," I say. And that's that.

It's the weirdest sleepover. In my own house, with my sister. Not excited, but sad. We lie in the darkness – Cat in her bed, me on the floor, each with our phones in our hands. Waiting. Waiting for the call that does not come. To tell us whether Gran has lived or died.

It's the longest night I've ever known.

I think I must have fallen asleep around dawn. It's late when I'm woken up by Cat, shuffling out of the room. I check my phone. Nothing.

"Mum!" I run to her room. "Any news?"

She's sitting up in bed, drinking coffee. "She's hanging on, Jess," Mum replies. "We'll all go and see her after breakfast if you like."

Back at the hospital, we file into the stuffy room once again. Dad's aged even more overnight. His clothes are crumply, his hair's not spiked up like normal. He almost looks like a regular dad.

"How is she?" Cat asks.

But Lauren pushes past her, her brown hair scraped into bunches. She takes Gran's lifeless hand in her small, chubby hand. "Don't die, Gran," she says.

And then it's not just me who's got tears in her eyes. Dad sits back down in his chair and sobs – big, man sobs.

"Daddy," scolds Lauren, "*you're* not poorly, so stop being silly. Stop being such a . . ." her faces scrunches up as she thinks of the right word. "Wanker," she says proudly. "Stop being such a wanker."

Dad blows his nose. "Right, kiddo, you said it. Time for Daddy to man up."

A thin voice whispers from the bed. "Well said, Lauren. Listen to the child, Stephen."

And that's the moment when I know my Gran is still very much in the building. She might be down but she's not out yet.

A few hours later, I'm sitting beside her bed, holding her hand. Mum's taken Lauren to nursery, Dad's gone home to sleep for a few hours, leaving Cat and me in charge. Doctor Flanagan's been in and checked Granny over. She seemed pleased. Granny couldn't speak much but her breathing's stronger and easier. Now's she's asleep but somehow she seems different from last night. I don't feel like she's slipping away from us any more.

Cat's outside, talking to Dad on her mobile. Then the door opens and she comes back in. "Dad'll come and pick us up later and then he's going to stay the night again," she tells me.

I nod and continue to stroke Gran's hand. "I can't stop thinking that this is our fault."

Cat shrugs. "People get old; we're not to blame. Anyway, Gran hardly lives a healthy life."

I don't like her criticising Gran. "I thought you'd approve. She eats even less than you."

"And makes up the calories in alcohol. It's a miracle that she's still alive."

Okay, that's enough. "Don't start on Gran," I say.

Cat softens her face. "I don't mean to be harsh, Jess. But everyone needs to take care of themselves. You can hardly expect to live a long and healthy life if you don't look after your body."

I feel there's a subtext to all this, a subtext that I don't like.

"Now's not the time for a sermon on healthy living. And especially not from you."

"Okay, I confess. Maybe I've taken not eating too far."

I stop looking at Gran and start looking at Cat. Am I hallucinating? Cat appears to be saying that maybe she is wrong. I'm not sure what to say. Perhaps I should meet her halfway.

"Maybe I take food too seriously. But the thing is, Cat, it's the one thing that I'm good at, the only thing that makes me different from everyone else. If I'm not Jess the food freak, I'm not sure who I am."

Cat nods. "I get that."

"But I'm beginning to think I need to find a middle ground. Enjoy food, but not be obsessive."

"Keep exercising with me and you can eat what you want."

Now that is an idea. I'm not sure it's a good idea, but it is an idea. Another one begins to form in my head.

"Between the two of us, we seem to have got things rather wrong. But between the two of us, we could have a solution."

She studies me carefully. "What do you mean?"

I smile a sad smile. "I mean, I'm fat sister; you're skinny sister. But you know how to exercise and I know how to cook."

She almost looks interested. "We could write a book. Or start a blog."

"I think I've had enough internet fame," I say but, even as I say it, I think that maybe this is a good idea. I mean, everyone has a blog nowadays. And we do have something to say. Something that other girls might actually listen to.

"Fair enough," she says. "But now I need coffee. Want some?"

I make a face. "It will be disgusting. But go on, I need something."

So off she goes to get me coffee. *Fat sister, skinny sister,* I think. There might be something in that. I smile for a moment, and just stop myself from thinking *I must tell Alex about that.* Because I can't tell Alex anything. Not as long as I want to keep Izzie as my friend.

I've made my choice.

And now I've just got to learn to live with it.

Chapter 30

Invisible Rule № 20: Boys have leadership skills, girls are bossy.

The next few days are a blur of school, visiting Gran and generally being a family. Which is very odd. Cat and Lauren talk to each other. Mum and Dad take turns at the hospital, being responsible. Dad still looks like he's just got out of bed and doesn't know what day of the week it is but he's starting to read a book about *How To Be the Perfect Carer*. At this point, I realise that I've never seen my dad read a book before.

And me . . . well, I bake healthy and nourishing food, discuss with my friends the next party and then the Prom, share revision plans and exam tips . . . and feel very, very alone.

Things are mostly the same a week later. But Gran is not breathing on a ventilator, she's up and chatting, asking for her old films and her special cigarettes. When we point out to her the hospital's non-smoking policy, she just gets cross and asks to be wheeled outside to escape from their oppressive, totalitarian regime. So we know that she's still with us.

There's a party this weekend. Dom is sixteen, the baby of our group. I forget he's younger than me, as he towers over me. I should be looking forward to it. Everyone else is. But what's the point? I can't be with Alex. He texted me a few times. I didn't reply. So he stopped texting altogether. I don't blame him. I can't explain the truth. I dread what he must be thinking about me – I must look like such a tease.

Maybe that's why I'm not hungry. I'm mean, there's something seriously wrong with me otherwise. I don't want to go to a party. I don't want to cook. I don't want to look at my phone. In fact I might as well be dead.

So it's Saturday night, and Hannah, Izzie and me are getting ready. But all I can think of is how much has changed since Matt's party. I've never felt like this before. It's a bit like your first Christmas after you've worked out that there's no Father Christmas and you're kind of like, well, what's the point of it all now?

So Hannah is curling her hair, Izzie is making her big eyes even bigger with a bit of help from her smoky-eyes kit, and frankly I'm bored. Yes, bored. Which again is not like me, cos I'm never bored. Life is generally just too damn interesting to be bored.

"Izzie," I say.

She hmms at me, deep in concentration, applying her fourth layer of mascara.

"Will you read my cards?"

She drops the mascara wand and eyes me with deep suspicion. "Why?" she asks.

Hannah is looking at me strangely too.

I don't want to say I'm bored cos that would just be rude. So I try a different angle.

"Well, then, you can tell me how my evening is likely to be and then I can see what it's actually like. Kind of like an experiment." I nod internally to myself. That almost sounds plausible.

"I'm not sure it works that way," Izzie says, one eye huge and smoky, one normal sized.

"Izzie, just for once I'm asking you to do a reading. Is that so hard to understand?"

She sniffs, but she reaches into her bag and draws out her rather battered pack of cards. She shuffles them, gets me to pick a random number, turns them over and thinks deeply. While I do think this is a load of old poo that I'm doing just to please her, I have to confess that the cards themselves are rather pretty.

In particular, I like the card I've turned over – the Queen of Wands, who looks kind of cool.

Izzie regards the cards carefully, and stares at me thoughtfully. Then she examines the cards again. She looks confused.

TBH I'm getting a bit worried now. "Don't tease me, Izzie," I say.

Hannah is also peering at the cards in concern. "What do they say? Is it something bad?" she asks.

I am now officially a bit freaked out. "What?" I ask with a bit more emphasis.

"Nothing, really," she says slowly.

"Well, 'nothing' is making you make some fairly frightening faces," I say.

"I think you're going to have a good evening," she says thoughtfully. "I think that something unexpected is going to happen."

"Which is . . .?" I say.

"Only time will tell," she says.

I'm sure she's keeping something from me. But what? The cards can't have actually told her anything, cos it's not real – it's just superstitious nonsense. I think . . .

But as Izzie puts her cards away, I can see her still looking at me and still thinking. I also see that there's no point saying anything to her.

Soon we're ready, and it's time to go. It's the same routine as last time for Matt's party. Same results but I'm hoping that the evening doesn't quite go as horrifically as last time. *Get over yourself, Jess*, I say to myself. *You're a teenager, it's Saturday night and you're going to a party full of your friends. Which bit of this is not okay?* But another part of me would rather be watching reruns of *MasterChef* on TV, laughing when they get their technique wrong.

We arrive at Dom's house, having run down the street as it's just started to rain. So we're all giggly and flushed as we knock on the door. Dom's family live in one of these little but incredibly expensive terraced houses which all look the same – everything inside is white, shiny or requires sunglasses before viewing properly. Dom hugs us all and then we follow him down to the super-cool basement where there's a v shiny kitchen (which I would KILL to have), a cool chill-out area and those fold-out doors into the garden. The one advantage of living round here is that I get to hang out in very nice houses. Though these generally show me how shabby my own house is. As I've said, I'm not a jealous person. Unless it's a very shiny kitchen. Have I mentioned that already?

So I help myself to a drink, chat to Sana and Bex who are standing next to the stereo, at that stage when their feet are tapping but they're not full-on dancing. So we put on our favourite track and start to dance properly. And I've forgotten how much fun it is to dance with your friends.

We dance for ages. I can feel my thigh, leg and stomach muscles from Cat's punishing workout. But it's not a bad pain. I just feel like I've used my body for once. But what I'm trying to say is, I need a rest. So I back out of the gaggle of girls who are now busting their moves and take some time out. I find myself standing next to Dom.

"Happy birthday," I say. "Good party." We look at the large group of teenagers, all drinking, chatting, laughing and dancing.

"Yeah," he nods happily, "this is good. Times like this I feel it's okay being us."

"Why? What gets to *you*?" I say. I wouldn't have thought that very much ever bothered Dom. He's sort of a Teflon guy – nothing sticks to him.

"You know, the usual – spots, getting good grades, my parents always comparing me to my sister and saying I don't work as hard, trying to get girls to like you."

And it's like a light bulb has gone on over my head. Here was me, thinking that girls had the hardest time, but I suppose much of what bothers us bothers them, just in a different kind of way.

I look at Dom's spots (without letting him see that's what I'm doing). They are kind of obvious. But a girl can wear make-up and try to hide them. All a boy can do is smile and pretend they don't bother him.

As I wonder how I can share this with him, my heart does a leap and then a somersault. A familiar tall figure has walked in. Alex.

My eyes flicker over his profile and, as his eyes turn to me, I listen intently to Dom but find it hard to concentrate because I'm too aware that Alex is in the room.

I don't look at him. But I can just feel that he's there. I want to look, to see what he's up to. But then I don't want to appear interested. God, this is confusing.

"Jess, are you listening to me?" Dom says with a smile.

"Yeah, I'm just . . . hungry!" I say. When in doubt, mention food! I'm not actually hungry, but somehow people always expect me to talk about food, so it's an easy excuse.

I allow myself a quick glance round the room.

Alex is talking to Izzie. They're standing, slightly away from everyone else. I can't see his face but I can see hers. And she's happy. Like she's standing in a spotlight. She gleams.

I think I'm going to be sick. You know I said I'm not a jealous person? Forget that.

I am.

And suddenly I realise what I've signed up for. I promised not to see Alex. But Izzie didn't promise the same. So if the two of them start something, then she won't have broken any agreement with me.

N
O
O
O
O
O
O
!!

I don't know whether Izzie manipulated that and I'm stupid for not seeing it. Or whether she never even thought of it. But, whatever, they're over there getting all friendly and I'm over here discussing the fact that Dom's mum forgot to buy him a cake.

The C-word gets my attention, despite my horror at what's happening over there.

"No cake?" I say, shocked.

"No cake," he repeats sadly. "She said she'll get me one tomorrow."

"You mean," I say, "that you're having a party. And we have no cake. This is an emergency."

Dom is clearly finding all this funny.

"Well, you're the cake girl. You could do something about it."

And at that moment, I nod my head. Yes, I could feel sorry for myself. Or, I could save the party, and distract myself by doing what I do best: I will make cake.

Jess Jones, Queen of Cakes, to the rescue.

I start rummaging through cupboards and generally making myself busy. I mean, it does start a burst of laughing and general comments of "Jess, what ARE you doing?" When I point out the terrible situation we are in – a party with no cake – people accept that yes, something needs to be done, and yes, I am the girl for the job. It might look a bit odd, making a cake at a party, but I am among friends. Who accept my weirdness. That is why they are called friends. End of.

It keeps me busy for an hour or so. And then the decoration. All the time, people come and chat to me. It's nice. It keeps me busy. And yes, I do let my eyes drift round the room from time to time. And yes, I can't help but notice that Izzie is still with Alex, though Hannah and Dom have joined them. It doesn't make me feel any better.

So I concentrate on making the cake look lovely. And by the time I've finished, it does. I mean, I've had limited time and resources so I couldn't make it quite the way I would normally, but I've iced the words to his favourite song over the top.

The time has come. I tell Hannah to put the right track on the iPod. The lights go off, the candles are lit. We sing "Happy Birthday" and Dom looks really, really happy. Looking round the circle of faces, *everyone* looks really happy. I'm not saying that I did all of that: but I did something that brought a smile to quite a few faces. And that's not a bad thing. I'll tell Cat about this when we have our next argument about food.

When the moment is over, I'm not quite sure what to do with myself.

I eat some cake and it's really nice. But what next? I get myself a drink and I wander out into the garden.

I like being outside on a warm, early summer evening. It feels like you're on holiday. I'd quite like to be on holiday from myself for a while.

There's someone standing next to me.

My heart jumps.

But it's Izzie.

I just wanted it to be . . . well, there's no use going there, but I wanted it to be someone else. Like Alex, for example.

"The cake was good," she starts. It feels a bit lame to me, but I go with it.

"I enjoyed making it," I say truthfully.

There's something up. She's shifting from side to side a bit.

I gulp. She's going to tell me that something's happened between her and Alex.

I'm not sure I can take this.

"Jess," she starts hesitantly, "I don't know quite how to say this."

"Then don't," I say lightly, trying to hide the strange mixture of anger and sadness that is churning around in me.

"I need to," she continues. "This is important."

I don't say anything. I just want to go home now. The thought of my bed is very appealing. It's very tiring, all this partying, baking, being emotional.

"Thing is," she says, "I think I've made a mistake."

Okay, I wasn't expecting that. She's got my interest now.

"I mean, not about the way I feel. I do really like Alex."

There's a terrible pause. I daren't say anything. I don't trust myself.

"But I think, what I asked you to do – I think that wasn't fair."

I'm in danger of suffocating. I don't trust myself to breathe just yet. Is she going to say what I think she's going to say?

"Jess, I've been thinking. In all the time we've been friends, you've been the best. Apart from Matt's party, you've only ever been amazing. And tonight, you made it really special, just to make Dom happy, just because you like him and you wanted to be nice. I can't think of what I do that's the same." She takes a deep breath and so do I, cos otherwise I'm gonna pass out.

"What I'm trying to say is, I don't think that you would have made me promise not to do anything with Alex, if it had been the other way round. And it's also pretty clear to me that Alex likes you. Not me. It was in your cards."

I love tarot cards. They are the best. Any fool who says they don't believe in them is a grade-A idiot.

I just about trust myself to speak now. "So . . ."

"If I'm really your friend, then I should want the best for you. So, if you do like Alex – go for it, Jess."

And that's the bit where I hug her. And she hugs back. And I might have a tear in my eye. Cos I think she's just been the best friend a girl could have.

"Thank you," I say, and I don't think I've ever meant two words as much as I mean those ones.

And now I don't know what to do.

It's one thing for Izzie to say that it's okay but it's another to do something about it. I mean, from Alex's point of view, my behaviour has been a bit weird. One minute we're snogging each other's faces off, the next minute I've gone cold on him.

What do I do? Just go up to him, jump on him and say, "Let's get it on?"

I come back into the party area and start to look around. At least if he's here I can try to talk to him and see what happens next.

Hannah notices my reappearance.

"If it's my brother you're after, he's gone," she says. "I think he thought there wasn't much point staying. He's just left."

"Oh," I say, and then I find myself walking out the front door.

The high street is busy with grown-ups swanning from one over-priced bar to the next. I look for Alex's tall figure among them.

Which way is he likely to have gone?

Most likely home, I think. That's where I'd want to be if I were in his situation.

I sort of jog down the road. I mean, not full-on running. Cos that would look weird and I don't have any of my three sports bras on me.

But I just have this feeling that I must see Alex tonight. I must try and get him to see that I'm not emotionally unstable. Or weird. That there was a good reason for all of this. I was trying to be a good friend.

Maybe it's just put him off me.

What will I say when I see him? *If* I see him.

I hurry through the darkening streets, thinking that possibly this wasn't one of my best ideas.

A hand grabs me on the shoulder and pulls me back.

I scream and spin round.

Alex. Holding a package of fish and chips in his other hand.

"Jones. What do you think you are doing?"

I catch my breath and steal one of his chips.

"Looking for you," I say.

"What's up? You looked like you were having a good time. Me, I've started comfort eating," he continues.

"Where's the vinegar?" I say. "You can't have chips without vinegar."

"I prefer ketchup," he says.

I wonder for a moment if all of this is for nothing. Can I really like a guy who puts ketchup on chips?

"But I could be persuaded on the merits of other condiments. Seriously, though, what are you doing?"

I take a deep breath. "Oh, you know – just looking for a guy with some chips to share."

I could tell him about Izzie, the promise, the cards. Or I could just eat chips with him and see where it goes.

"Well, fortune's smiling on us both. I was looking for a girl to eat chips with."

I smile at him – a real, honest, big smile.

And at some point, the chips disappear. And at some point, we might kiss. And at some point, some other stuff might happen.

But I don't want to tell you about that.

Cos, for once, it's none of your business!

I think it's time for a new chapter. ☺

Chapter 31

Jess Observation № 10: Rom-coms are all very well, but the only reason that they have happy endings is cos of where the film ends. Three weeks later it could be a whole different story. That's the bit when they both realise that the reason they fought for the first three quarters of the film was because they really did hate each other. Now the sex is out of the way, there's nothing else to distract them from this.

So, a week later. This is happiness.

It's late on Saturday night. And we've not gone out.

Did you like the way I dropped a "we" in there?

We're lying in my bed. Just lying there. That's all. Sometimes that's the best bit. Just being close and warm. I can feel him breathing, hear his heart beating.

And the best bit is – this is where he wants to be. With me. Cos I'm me.

And we're not at a party, showing off that we're . . . well, together. Cos I've still got Izzie to think of. And cos it wouldn't be cool.

So instead we're here. Watching a cool film, talking, laughing, just hanging out. And it feels amazing.

So what have the last seven days been like?

1. I have kissed and been kissed every day.
2. Yes, I have thought of Matt from time to time, but though Matt might look like he's perfect, Alex actually is close to perfect so far. Izzie is a bit sad and quiet but apparently the cards are telling her something good is on the horizon. So that's okay.
3. Hannah thinks it's all very bizarre but it's okay cos I don't have to talk to her about what we do. Especially as it involves her brother.

4. Gran's doing okay. She's still in hospital, but she's much better than she was. We have a rota to sit with her while she eats the odd mouthful. We're doing better looking after her.

5. I've heard Mum on the phone to her friends, talking about me having a boyfriend. She's a mixture of proud, amazed and relieved. I think that she's dying for me to ask her advice about something, but I'm not going to do it just yet. I'll save that one up for when I want her to buy me some very expensive ingredients.

6. Alex has been introduced to Alice and Lauren. Now I'm not saying that it's love yet, but a guy who's prepared to tolerate your four-year-old sister's imaginary friend must be pretty much okay.

7. Dad and Alex just discuss guitar chords, so this avoids any potential awkwardness that might arise between Dad's sworn duty to protect his children and Alex's appreciation for pretty much every part of my body.

8. Word has spread at school about me and Alex and, while Zara still looks at me as if I'm made out of dog poo, I did have a nice image in my head of me turning up to the Prom with Alex next to me. Ha! Take that, skinny girl!

So generally, all round, everyone I care about is okay and I'm okay. For the first time in weeks, since that stupid Own Clothes Day.

I breathe a happy sigh.

I've been so busy thinking over all the good stuff that's been going on, I've not been listening to Alex. Bad girlfriend.

So I tune back in, start randomly agreeing with him till I've worked out what he's going on about.

"Did you actually hear what I just said?" Alex says.

I decide to be honest. "Not entirely. I was just enjoying the sound of your voice." Well, *nearly* honest.

"And what were you thinking about that was so important?"

I decide to be a bit more honest now. I mean, apparently honesty is the basis of proper relationships. But I think that's more grown-up relationships. Teenage relationships are pretty much based on hormones, music and alcohol.

But I decide to be brave.

"I was thinking about what we should wear to the Prom."

Then Alex looks at me as if I've said something really stupid. I mean, I know it's not like me to think about clothes – but he's not going to dump me for that, is he? Oh God, what have I done?

"Jess, you weren't listening to me at all, were you?"

"Maybe not," I flounder. Is that really such a bad thing, to let your mind wander when someone's talking to you? Is there a book about how to be a perfect girlfriend somewhere? Maybe I should read it. I think my mind's wandering again. Or is it panic?

"I was telling you about my training weekend, the one I'm going on in preparation for my expedition."

"Ye-e-ss?" I agree, still feeling like I've very much missed the point here.

Alex looks more gently at me this time.

"And the weekend is next weekend. So that makes it . . ."

I get it now. And my heart sinks. ". . . the same weekend as the Prom."

"You got it. I'm sorry, Jess, but I can't come to the Prom with you."

There is silence. I mean, yes, I'm disappointed. Yes, a bit of me did want to prove Zara wrong. I was going to show all her little crowd and just general idiots that even me, even a girl who is less than plastic perfect, can be liked and not be a loser. But I was also looking forward to Alex coming with me because he's Alex and I'm Jess and I think we sort of go together.

I'm not sure how much of this to share.

"I'm sorry, Jess," he says, holding me closer again. "I can't get out of it, and even if I could, I didn't think that you were really into proms. I mean, it's not really your thing, is it . . .?"

As his voice trails off, I know why he says that. I mean, it's all dresses, and showing off, fake tans, false nails, false boobs and goodness knows what else. But I do want to go, to have a good night with my friends. And just now, it won't be the same without him.

"Are you crying?" he says, and pulls my chin up to check.

"Hayfever," I say, and wipe my tears and his hand away. "You're right. It's a stupid night. I was just looking forward to it."

"It's just one weekend."

"But then you're away for four weeks."

"But I'm coming back, Jess. And then we've got the rest of the summer."

And that is true. And when I get over my disappointment, I will be happy about that.

But not yet. So when he starts to kiss me, I kiss back. But sadly.

Chapter 32

Jess Observation № 11: Mums can be useful. Sometimes.

I'm standing in the too-shiny marbled interior of our nearest oversized shopping centre and I'm having a revelation. For years, I've wondered about where all the fat people are. Cos they don't live round where I live. And I know that there are fat people out there cos they're always in the news for being fat and dying too young. But I never see very many. And now I know. They come to the Trafford Centre.

It's such a relief. I see a girl my age, my size, and part of me wants to rush up to her and hug her and go, "There you are! A fellow fat person . . . we must have so much in common."

That wouldn't be a good idea on so many levels. But I do feel better. Cos all these fat people are well dressed and look reasonable, not as if they're gorging themselves on fast food in front of fifty-six-inch HD TVs while claiming benefits, which is what most people generally seem to think about fat people. As if fat people weren't just ordinary people. Who ate a bit too much.

I sigh. I think, after this amazing revelation, that the rest of the day can only go downhill.

"Here's your salted caramel mocha, Jess," Mum says. I sip, enjoy and decide not to tell Cat about this. She wouldn't approve. But if I've got to go dress shopping for the Prom then I need something wonderful to keep me going.

So all in all, this isn't looking good.

1. I don't like shopping.
2. I don't like the Trafford Centre.
3. Alex can't come to the Prom with me.
4. Alex can't come to the Prom with me.

I know I put that twice, but that's cos it's twice as bad as anything else on the list.

And while it's fab that Mum is here to help me – cos if anyone can find a dress that make me looks all right it's her – it does limit how much I can talk about Alex. And I can't talk to Izzie because – well, you can see why not. And Hannah has just started a really good book so she won't leave the house until she's finished.

So it's Sunday – a day I could have spent cooking a really nice meal for my family – but instead I'm stuck inside in a fake neo-classical edifice that's dedicated to clothes, labels and most things I think are rubbish. Joy.

"Let's just get on with it," I sulk.

Mum fixes me with a hard stare. "That is not the right spirit. Most girls would think this is fun."

I just sulk even more. She breathes in deeply. "Now don't bite my head off, but we need to know what size to shop for."

TBH I havn't much thought about what size I am any more. But then I think that what with the healthy eating, being too stressed to eat, and Cat's Nazi-style boot camp, then I can't have put weight on.

"Don't worry – no tape measures. After a lifetime of fashion experience, I think I can tell just by looking at you."

With that in mind, I plaster a fake smile on my face and let her lead me on.

And after a bit I do start to enjoy myself. I mean, some of the clothes in the shops ATM are quite funny. See-through tops? Which pervert thought that was a good idea? And the shoes . . . well, you'll know what I mean, but how are you supposed to wear them? Mum and I try on quite a few pairs and keep falling over until the shop assistant throws us out cos it is quite clear that we aren't going to buy anything. I don't think she likes the fact that we think they are funny. Apparently, Fashion is *serious*. Fashion doesn't do funny. Which is a shame. Cos I do like to laugh.

But then Mum makes me shop properly. To be fair, she has really thought about it. She's researched which shops have sizes, cuts and colours to suit me. She shows me a range of clothes she's pre-selected on her phone and then we go to the shops to see them in the flesh.

I mean, my heart isn't in it. My heart is still debating which is worse – the fact that Alex isn't coming to the Prom with me or that Alex is going away for four weeks of the summer holiday. Part of me wants him to go, "No, the Prom is important to you. I'll give up my life's ambition of travelling to Peru just for a party." But part of me doesn't. Because then I'd just be being selfish. And that's not the kind of person that I want to be.

"So – this one or this one?"

I snap back into the present. Mum is holding up two gorgeous dresses on their hangers, one dark blue, one violet. The violet one looks a bit like the one Mum bought me before.

"The blue," I say, without much conviction.

So I find that I'm shoved in a cubicle with a long mirror that's far too close to me for my liking, and expected to remove my clothes.

I think about my options. Whether I could wear something I already have. Apparently that's not allowed. I've put my foot down over the spray tan, false nails etc. I might let Hannah near me with fake lashes, but that's it.

So I strip down to my pants and put the dress on.

It doesn't stick or cling anywhere.

The zip goes up smoothly.

With my eyes screwed up, I turn towards the mirror.

I take a deep breath and open them.

It's okay.

It's more than okay.

I turn round. It fits, and it looks good.

I mean, I'm still me. I've still got my boobs and my hips and my thighs. I'm sure Cat would still think I'm fat. But I look at myself long and hard and think, *Well, yes, I think I look nice.*

Shyly, I pull back the curtain and show Mum.

Her face confirms what I was thinking. As she fusses over me, I enjoy the moment. And that's a good feeling. It's okay being me. It really is.

She wants to know if I want to try on the other dress. But I've chosen now. This dress likes me and I like it.

Now time for lunch, to celebrate. Mum lets me choose. There are loads of restaurants, but they're all a bit plastic, if you know what I mean. But I choose a place that does great burgers, partly cos I think they'll be good but partly because I want to see Mum's reaction. That might seem a bit mean, but I can't help wanting to see how *Mum vs. Burger* plays out.

I choose one with cheese and bacon but I decide not to eat the bun. I mean, you just don't need it and it doesn't even taste nice. Mum has a "naked" burger. That doesn't mean it's pornographic – it just doesn't have anything extra on it, to make it even tastier. I think we're both happy with our choices.

As we're eating (me chomping and commenting on every mouthful, Mum delicately nibbling) Mum says to me, "This blog of yours . . ."

I nearly spit out my burger. "What blog?" I say. Cos I haven't actually done anything, it was just an idea.

"Cat mentioned it last night. I think it would be a good idea." Mum continues to eat her burger, one nano-particle at a time. "You do have a real talent for cooking and baking, Jess. You should try and do something with that."

I'm blushing now. And confused. I mean, not only is Mum being helpful, SHE'S ENCOURAGING ME TO EAT. I feel like running out to see if the sun is still up in the sky, or whether the world has ended and my mum has been replaced by an alien.

"Thanks," is all I manage, which is not particularly articulate but it's all I can do at the moment.

And I get a lovely warm feeling inside. It's just such a relief not to be fighting with Mum.

That's when I have a revelation. I'm going to try being nice to people who have pissed me off. Then I'll feel okay about myself and I'll mess with their minds at the same time. I mean, how other people react to kindness is up to them.

Maybe niceness rocks after all.

Chapter 33

Invisible Rule № 21: Skinny girls are attractive, skinny boys are geeks; muscly guys are hot, muscly girls are butch.

So . . .

Alex has gone. That's that then.

I had a proper boyfriend for two weeks. I mean, it's not as if it's all over. But he's gone for the weekend. And then he's off for four weeks. Which is a long time.

I feel sort of hollow inside. Like one of those rubbish Easter eggs without any treats in it. And I'm not just hollow, I'm restless too. Then I think about Gran. She's still got an oxygen cylinder to help with her breathing when she needs it, but she's well enough to stay at home with us.

Doctor Flanagan began to talk to Dad about how to look after her, but there wasn't any need. You can just see by looking at him that Dad's decided that Things Are Going To Change.

Change Number One. Granny is not up on the top floor on her own. No, we've sorted her out a room downstairs, so someone is always wandering in and out. We never used the back sitting room anyway. And it's next to the kitchen so it's easier than ever to bring her food and she's promised that she might even join us to eat from time to time.

I go in to see her, armed with a pot of tea and two mugs.

She's coughing loudly as I knock.

"Jess, love," she says with relief. "Go and get me some of your father's tobacco, will you?"

"No," I reply. "Get it yourself if you want it."

She gives me a hard stare.

"With these old legs?"

I give her a hard stare back. "I'm not helping you to consume poison. That's what put you in hospital."

She coughs again. "I'm too old to change now, Jesobel.

You've got to see that."

I am not moved. "That's no attitude. You're only in your seventies. You could make it to a hundred if you just took a bit better care of yourself."

"This is becoming a boring conversation," Gran says. "If I continue to be bored I will return to my attic. Now tell me something more interesting and distract me from my nicotine withdrawal. What's going on with you? At one point you were cavorting half dressed in some kind of video. And last time we spoke, I distinctly remember that you'd been sending dubious pictures via your telephone—"

I blush and interrupt her. "There's been no more of that! And as for the clip . . ." I think for a moment about it. "I think that was just my fifteen minutes of fame. In fact, it didn't even last that long." Then, shyly, I begin to tell her about Alex, Izzie, the various cakes and pies, and about how Alex can't come to the Prom with me.

She listens carefully. "Well, you have been busy. I still don't see what all the fuss was about this boy though. You and Izzie, you're still good friends then?"

I nod.

"Well then," she cracks with laughter, "you should have just shared him. Sisterly solidarity!"

"Granny," I snap back, "he's not a box of chocolates! I don't want to share him with anyone."

She sighs. "You do have very conformist tendencies at times. I do worry about you." I'm about to follow this up when she continues, "This Prom. I don't really like the sound of it. It sounds hideous."

"It's a good job it's me who's going then, not you," I reply. "I know what you mean, but I'll be there with my friends, we'll be having fun. It's the end of an era. I've been at that school for five years. That's why it's so important."

"Perhaps. But if that's what it's all about, then it seems to me that it doesn't make a jot of difference if you have a boy with you or not."

I know she's right. But I did really want to share it with Alex too . . .

She looks at me with her sharp, bright eyes.

"I know you're a bit down now but I have to say that in general you have seemed happier this last week or so. Once you recovered from fussing over me." As I try to say something, she waves a hand at me to stop me talking. "I hope you haven't got it into your head that a boy equals happiness."

I think about this. "No, not any boy. But Alex's really nice." Now it's my turn to silence Gran. "I know that it probably won't last forever. But now it's good. And he seems to like pretty much everything about me. So I'm just enjoying the moment really." Pausing for a moment to collect my thoughts, I continue, "I thought I had to choose between my friend and Alex, but in the end it turns out I can have both."

Granny nods and gives me a wink. "Well, I think that's called having your cake and eating it. Though I've never seen what the point is of having cake if you're not allowed to eat it. Now, given you're so wise and grown up, how about getting your old granny something she likes? If you don't get it, I'll send Lauren to find it. I'll tell her Alice told me to tell her."

"You are not using Lauren as a drugs mule," I protest.

"Watch me try," she says with a glint in her eye.

I leave the room, shaking my head but smiling.

It's good to have her back.

Chapter 34

Jess Observation on Invisible Rules № 1: Sometimes rules are useful. Sometimes they are there to be broken. You just need to pick and choose. Like a pick'n'mix. Only less calorific.

So we're getting ready. Again. Haven't we all been here before . . .?

But there are some changes. First, Sana and Bex are also rocking the place with us. Sana's dad has a cool car and so he's taking us. Mum offered to get us a limo but that's so not cool.

I'm a bit sad. I can still feel Alex's goodbye kiss last night. I mean, he'll be back tomorrow, so it's not the Big Goodbye that's in a few weeks. So I'm not sad about that. But it would have been good to have shared tonight with him.

But then I look around the room. The music is thumping, every socket has got some appliance plugged into it. I mean, hair straighteners, curling wands, that kind of thing . . .

And the room is full of my friends. And we're happy and we're going to enjoy ourselves this evening.

By now, I think you know the routine. Are my legs still smooth? Yes, not because anyone else is going to touch them but just cos that's the way I want them to be tonight.

Soon, we're dressed, made up, with perfect hair. We pose for photos, endless selfies in different combinations. I pity the mobile phone network in this area.

There's a knock at the door.

"That'll be my dad," Sana says. "God, is that the time?"

Hannah opens the door and does a half scream. "That's so freaky!"

We all turn to look as a tall, lanky figure ambles through the door. It's wearing a mask.

"But . . ." I start. "What . . ."

Cos someone is standing in the cellar door, wearing a mask of Alex's face. Which you have to admit is pretty weird.

For a moment I think about whether Alex himself is playing a strange trick on me. But then the mask is pulled off and Dom's spotty face is revealed beneath.

"What's all this about?" I say.

"Alex knew you were upset about him not coming, so I'm going to be him tonight. Not in all respects, of course – Alex was very clear on what I was and was not allowed to do." Dom grins wickedly and I blush fiercely. "But I'm to escort you, dance with you and not leave your side all night."

"It's kind of creepy, but I like it," I say.

"It's so cute," Bex says.

Izzie doesn't say anything. But she does smile at me, so I think that that's okay. Sort of.

But before any of us can think about it too much, Sana's dad is here in his massive Range Rover, all decorated with rainbow ribbons the way we wanted – not just girly pink for us. So with all us girls strapped in and Dom in the boot, music blaring, we drive up the hill to school for our final party. Our last night as proper Year Elevens of St Etheldreda's School.

And school is the same, and yet all so different at the same time. The cars line up – yep, someone got a limo, there's a few Rolls Royces, about three jeeps. We get out, wave goodbye to Sana's dad and make our way into the gym.

It's been transformed. Instead of a dull, sweaty hall, where generations of students have been tortured, it's full of lights, music and balloons, and every possible surface is swagged and festooned with material, like some low-rent wedding reception.

And we're transformed too. Freed from our blazers, regimented skirts, blouses and jumpers, we're a glorious rainbow of colours. And while most of us have gone down the conventional dress route, one or two girls have turned up in full Goth outfit. Which is cool. I mean, if you can't please yourself tonight, then when can you?

One thing that hasn't changed is the teachers. Mr Ambrose and Mrs Brown stand like birds of prey, raking us with their eyes. But tonight is not their night. I look at Mrs Brown's hard, bitter face. I think back to what she said to me a few weeks ago and how I thought I'd burst from the injustice of it all.

Now . . .now . . . I'm just not that bothered what she thinks of me. I'm off to a new college and a new set of teachers. And what sort of life does she have if her only pleasure is tormenting girls? But tonight is not a night to think about teachers. Tonight is all about FUN with my friends.

We drift outside.

"It's beautiful," Hannah sighs. And it is. Underneath a resplendent summer sky, the green lawn is dotted with tents and gazebos, all linked with fairy lights and bunting in jewel-bright colours, fluttering in the wind. Groups of giddy girls and boys flit around, watching a magician here, trying different foods there, posing for a photo from time to time. Everyone is smiling.

"Come on." Izzie pulls me by the hand. "They're about to start." And I don't know what she's going on about until we reach the massive bean bags outside, all in front of a band who are about to play. It's like being at a mini-festival. (Though I don't think big hair, fake tans and posh frocks are generally the thing at festivals.)

And whose band is it? Well, Zara's pacing up and down as Matt and Co tune up. Yep, it should have been Alex playing but he's not. But Dom goes and stands there with him with his Alex mask on. Matt laughs at him and leans over for a chat. Zara zaps me with her disapproval as the band start to play.

And it's good, they're really good. I can't help but look at Matt. I mean, he's like a god walking among us. He really should be in a real band, a proper band. And as he sings, his eyes lock on mine for a moment and we both smile. I look at Zara. She should be happy. She's probably wearing the most expensive dress at the prom, but she doesn't look better than anyone else. She looks miserable. And angry. And that sort of makes her look ugly. And I sort of feel sorry for her. Where are her crowd?

She's the colour of mahogany, with nails like talons, and eyelashes so long that they keep getting stuck to her cheeks. She's just standing there on the side, wanting us to think how great she is cos she's with the band. But we're all together, laughing, having fun, and the band are looking at us, enjoying us enjoying their music. Dom is dancing away at the side like a crazy guy, pretending to play a guitar.

I turn to Izzie. "This is all crazy!" Then I lower my voice and ask gently, "You know the Alex mask . . .? Are you okay with all this, cos I'll stop it if you're not?"

But Izzie smiles back. "My cards are looking good. I'm not sure when it's going to happen but it's soon. I can wait until then."

And she seems to mean it. Which is good.

After a great set, the guys call it quits. We whoop, yell and shout for more songs. They'll be back later, but now it's time to dance.

We move back inside to the dance floor. I notice Tilly and Tiff, Lara and Sara all around, all mingling with other people, all having fun. I smile. I'm glad, cos that's what I'm having. I mean, I'm with my friends – what more could a girl want?

It's about then that I notice that Matt is on the dance floor, doing some kind of rock dance. And he keeps looking over at me. Zara is far away, looking daggers, looking miserable.

He edges closer to us. But then Alex's face gets between us. Dom's put the mask back on and dances close to me. He turns to Matt and waves a finger at him. "No way, not a chance." Matt just laughs and keeps dancing.

I can't help but look at Zara.

I take a deep breath and walk up to her.

"Come and dance, Zara," I find myself saying.

She looks amazed. "Why? So you can push me over?"

"Don't start, Zara. Look, it's our last Year Eleven night. Come and enjoy yourself. By the way, you look great tonight. But then you always do."

Zara doesn't know what to say. So she just pouts and says nothing. I shrug and leave her. I tried.

But later, I see she's dancing and before long she's found her way back to Matt's side. And then they're both smiling. And that's good. Cos now's the time for the Year Photo.

"Get in! Everyone together." Everyone on the dance floor crowds together and smiles for the camera.

And I think I'm smiling the most. Cos I know that when I see the photo, I'm going to see a girl smiling at me. And I think she's kind of cool and looks kind of nice.

And I'm her and she's me.

And that's just tickety-boo.

Acknowledgements

I used to think that writing was a solitary activity and didn't require the input of others. How very wrong I was!

I am indebted to all those I've met at the Writing School at Manchester Metropolitan University; firstly to Sherry Ashworth for offering me a place and for setting the writing exercise that gave birth to Jesobel, and my other writing tutors, Catherine Fox and Nicky Browne; secondly to the Scooby Gang: the most talented and supportive group of writers - Chrissy Dentan, Jason Hill, Kim Hutson, Matt Killeen, Luci Nettleton, Alison Padley-Woods, Katy Simmonds and Paula Warrington.

Next I have to thank my husband Dave for bringing wine to the study and for helping me in my hour of need: formatting. My children did get in the way of writing occasionally. Beth once said, "I want to help you to be a better writer." I replied that half an hour of peace would help. She snorted and said, "Well that's never going to happen."

This novel would never have seen the light of day without the support of my lovely agent Anne Clark who saw potential in Jesobel and helped me find the heart of the story.

And finally my thanks go to all the students I have taught over the years. I wouldn't have been able to write this with you!

Anna Mainwaring, November 2014

You can find out more about Jesobel (and me) at annamainwaring.com or annamainwaring1@twitter.com